JOURNEY OF
A THOUSAND MILES

Of course Lee had heard about the boat people –
they were heroes. But his own family's decision to
escape from Vietnam was a different matter. The
dangers of the sea voyage were enormous. Half the
boat people who left Vietnam were never heard of
again. In Lee's rickety fishing-boat forty people
were crammed tightly together. First came the
patrol launches, with orders to sink all refugee
craft and pick off survivors with rifles; then the
merciless pirates, looking for valuables and ready
to kill to get them. Passing ships continually
ignored their pleas for help. And for Lee and his
shipmates there was the battle against seasickness,
hunger and thirst – and always, the treacherous
South China Sea.

Award-winning author Ian Strachan brings this
extraordinary story to life through the eyes of Lee
and Chi, a boy and a girl who face up to the hazards
– and the challenges – of an incredible journey to
find a new life in freedom.

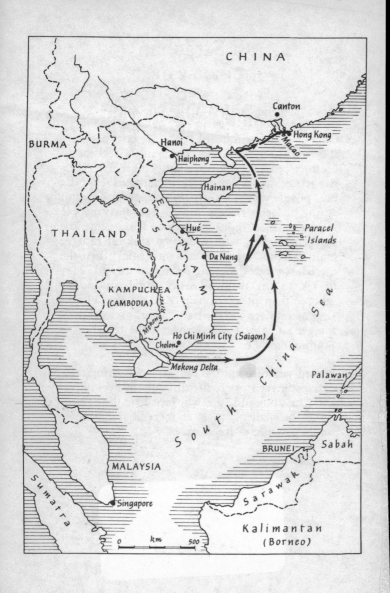

Ian Strachan

JOURNEY OF
A THOUSAND MILES

MAMMOTH

Also by Ian Strachan

The Boy in the Bubble
The Flawed Glass
Pebble of the Beach
The Second Step
throwaways
Wayne Loves Custard?

Poem published in *The Boat People*
by Bruce Great by Penguin Books 1979

Map references by Jo Strachan

First published in Great Britain 1984
by Methuen Children's Books Ltd
Magnet paperback edition published 1985
Reissued 1991 by Mammoth
an imprint of Reed Consumer Books Limited
Michelin House, 81 Fulham Road, London SW3 6RB
and Auckland, Melbourne, Singapore and Toronto

Reprinted 1991, 1992, 1993 (twice), 1995

Text copyright © 1984 Ian Strachan

ISBN 0 7497 0656 2

A CIP catalogue record for this title
is available from the British Library

Printed and bound in Great Britain
by Cox & Wyman Ltd, Reading, Berkshire

This book, which was written with the help of a bursary from West Midlands Arts, is dedicated not only to all the Vietnamese refugees but to all people all over the world, who are forced to abandon their homes and seek a new life, and to the organisations and individuals such as UNICEF, UN High Commissioner for Refugees, the Red Cross, Save the Children Fund and Ockenden Venture, who offer help where others will not.

'The journey of a thousand miles begins with one step.'

Lao-Tsze
The Simple Way

A Prayer for Land

Lost in the tempests
Out on the open seas
Our small boats drift.
We seek for land
During endless days and endless nights.
We are the foam
Floating on the vast ocean.
We are the dust
Wandering in endless space.
Our cries are lost
In the howling wind.
Without food, without water
Our children lie exhausted
Until they cry no more.
We thirst for land
But are turned back from every shore.
Our distress signals rise and rise again
But the passing ships do not stop.
How many boats have perished?
How many families lie beneath the waves?
Lord Jesus, do you hear the prayer of our flesh?
Lord Buddha, do you hear our voice
From the abyss of death?
O solid shore,
We long for you!
We pray for mankind to be present today!
We pray for land to stretch its arms to us!
We pray that hope be given us
Today, from any land.

*A poem written by an unknown Vietnamese
at a refugee camp in 1978.*

ONE

'Wake up! Wake up!'

The urgent whisper penetrated the dark layers of Lee's sleep. Reluctantly he swam up through them to open one eye. A torch-beam shone directly into it. The sharp pain made him snap it shut but the light still projected a dull, red glow through his closed lids.

'Lee!' his father hissed. 'You must wake up!'

'Why?' Lee mumbled. He struggled away from the bony fingers roughly shaking his shoulder.

'Get up as quickly as possible and get dressed.'

'What time is it?' Lee asked trying to drift back.

'Just gone midnight,' his father replied with a final shake. 'No more questions. Do as I say.'

Lee forced himself to sit up, rubbed his eyes and was surprised to find himself waking in his grandfather's cottage instead of the Cholon flat. As light from the torch swung across the room he realised Kim, his eldest sister, was already dressed and leaving while father was turning his attention to little Tam who slept on the small mattress in the corner.

Tam hated being woken at any time. She panicked at having her private world disturbed so abruptly, so that Lee was not surprised, as he fought his way into a sweater, to hear her muffled squawks of protest like a bird being pulled from its nest. By the time he was pulling on his jeans, the squawks had changed to whimpering cries but Lee knew they would dry up quickly enough. He was also well aware that his father, a dry and careful man, would not have woken them without good reason.

Lee found the rest of the family, Kim, mother, grandmother and, the head of the Nguyen family, grandfather, crammed into the tiny kitchen, lit only by the flickering light from a stump of candle. The room was stuffy and airless. Nobody looked up as he found a place. Instead they stared intently at two large lumpy bundles done up in black cloth as if they expected them to move at any moment.

Grandmother's eyes were red-rimmed from crying. That and the mysterious bundles, which all but smothered the table, were the only clues Lee needed to know they were about to try to leave Vietnam for ever.

Rumours of people leaving by boat had been rife at school, circulated mainly by boys whose parents listened to reports on foreign radio stations. Then one night a whole family disappeared from the block of flats where Lee's family lived in Cholon. Next day the word was they had set out on a boat bound for Singapore.

Ever since that day Lee had thought of little else but, hard as life had been since the departure of the Americans, for whom his father worked, Lee could never see him following their example. He was a solicitor, not only by training but also by nature. The most careful, circumspect man it seemed to Lee, he even chose his breakfast as if contemplating litigation, which made the present decision all the more surprising.

Lee felt his stomach sway with excitement as if he were already at sea as he tried to get used to the idea. His brain boiled over with questions he longed to ask but the stern expression on his grandfather's lean face indicated this was no time to speak out of turn.

The old man sat very still, examining his fisherman's fingers splayed out like sausages on the table before him. The fine lines which formed a network across his face, like the irregular cracks in dried mud, seemed deeper than usual in the yellow light of the candle.

The tense atmosphere was broken by Tam's arrival. She burst into the room just ahead of her father. There was no trace of the tears she had shed, instead her smooth oval face glistened with excitement as she rushed round the room in sheer pleasure, stumbling over ankles, until her mother hauled her up onto her knee to quiet her.

'Grandfather has something to tell us,' father said when they were all seated.

The old man looked up for the first time and Lee was once more startled, as always, by the intensity of his eyes, which always seemed to focus on a spot just inside your eyeball when he looked at you.

'We are going out for a walk,' he announced quietly.

'But it's dark,' Tam protested.

Lee shushed her irritably. Even at six she must realise what's going on.

'When we go outside,' grandfather carried on as if there had been no interruption, 'nobody must make the slightest sound. I know the path we must take best so I will lead with grandmother, and we will set the pace. The rest of you follow in pairs at regular intervals so that we don't lose sight of each other, but we will keep a few metres between us. Your mother and Kim go next....'

'What about me?' Tam cried out, anxiously bobbing about at the thought of being left out.

'I'll carry you,' mother replied.

'I'm too old to be carried!' Tam protested and looked as if she might cry again.

'But it's very dark outside,' mother pointed out, 'and we wouldn't want you to get lost.'

Faced with that choice, Tam fell silent.

'Lee and your father will be the last to leave,' grandfather continued. Lee felt a slight glow of pride, which faded a little when grandfather added, 'In case anybody follows us.'

Normally nothing upset Kim but at these words she began to look a little uncertain.

'You never know who's about at this time of night,' he murmured.

'Is there time for me to write a letter, grandfather?' she asked.

He shook his head slowly. 'No, Kim.'

'But I only want to write a note to Dong,' she pleaded.

Grandfather, who had said his last words on the subject, didn't bother to repeat them but father explained quickly, 'The fewer people who know what we're doing the better, Kim.' Tam looked totally mystified and wondered why all this fuss about a midnight walk? Lee just thought Kim was being stupid, thinking about writing a letter to her boyfriend at a time like this, and wondered why nobody seemed as excited as he was at the prospect of this great adventure.

'That,' father added quietly, 'is why we haven't told you until this moment. So that nobody could give anything away by accident, and if we are successful you will be able to write, Kim, and if not ...' His voice trailed away as he spread his long, thin hands in a gesture of hopelessness.

Grandfather, who could only tolerate so much modern democracy, cut in. 'I think it is time for us to go.'

Grandmother obediently rose and, grasping one of the black bundles firmly by the knot which held it together, swung it up on to her thin shoulders. Lee was always surprised, because she looked so old and frail, that she could carry such weights without staggering, but despite her years her body was mainly sinew and muscle.

Grandfather licked his thumb and forefinger to pinch out the candle flame. It died with a slight hiss. As Lee's eyes were growing accustomed to the dark he heard the creak of the cottage door as it swung open, briefly saw the outline of his grandparents against the night sky, then it swung shut and they were gone. At that moment, Lee realised, the adventure he had dreamt about had not only become a reality but also, from this point, there could be no drawing back from the events which lay ahead.

TWO

The sliver of new moon was barely enough to turn the narrow sandy track into a grey ribbon that meandered between the ramshackle cottages of the village. Somewhere hidden among them, a single dog barked. There was no message in its noise only a desperate attempt to persuade itself it was still alive in this desolate hour.

Lee could just make out the distorted shapes of his mother and Kim at the far end of the track. His mother had Tam on her back and Kim, despite being sixty-five years younger than grandmother, was stumbling under the weight of the second black bundle.

There were no lights showing in any of the cottages but Lee knew that the slightest noise could wake one of the sleeping occupants, who might be only too pleased to report them to the soldiers guarding the harbour. During the last six years, since the fall of Saigon, it had been hard to know whom you could trust.

In his anxiety to be quiet, Lee tripped over a stone and would have fallen full-length in the dust but for his father, who shot out a hand to save him.

Although the village did look unfamiliar in this curious light, Lee was convinced that Kim and their mother were going the wrong way, leading them away from the harbour where the boats were. Frantically he tugged at his father's arm and gestured towards the harbour but father shook his head emphatically and indicated they should keep going.

As they passed the last cottage, they turned off the main track down a narrower, winding path which, Lee knew from previous expeditions, led towards the paddy fields at the back of the village. Far off he could hear a water-buffalo grumbling in its throat.

Soon Lee found himself sliding down a steep bank.

At the bottom he felt the cool, muddy water oozing up beneath his jeans, right up to the knee. It was impossible to move quietly. Every step sent out a confusion of ripples across the moonlit surface that lapped at the rice tufts. The mud sucked at the soles of his shoes, reluctant to let him go any further.

Suddenly a dim light swept out briefly across the paddy. Lee instantly squatted beside his father, their heads pressed against the sandy bank as they heard the tinny clank of a bicycle being pedalled along the top of the dyke towards them.

Lee looked out across the water and was relieved to see the tell-tale ripples had died down to an indeterminate shimmer of movement.

Crouched down in the murky water Lee wondered who was on the bike. It might have been a fisherman or farmer on his way back from the next village but it could just as easily be a soldier on his way to relieve the sentry at the harbour. If it was a soldier and he caught them crouched down in a paddy field at this time of night, he wouldn't hesitate to shoot.

As the sound of the loose chain clanked slowly nearer, it was joined by the noise of the bell rung by the bike's vibration as it picked its way along the bumpy track. Loud as it was, Lee thought the sound of their breath seemed louder and then he got an overwhelming desire to cough.

Lee held his breath and swallowed hard several times but the irritating tickle remained. He held his breath, burying his face in his arm to deaden the sound if the worst should happen. Only when his lungs were aching from lack of oxygen, and he thought he would burst, did the cough disappear as quickly as it had come, leaving him trying to gulp in air as quietly as possible.

As Lee looked up, the shadow of the rider, cast by the moon across the water, was almost upon them. His father was twisting round trying to get a glimpse of the man above them. Lee was about to do the same, in spite

14

of an awful feeling that if he could see the man then the man would be able to see him too, when he felt something brush against his leg and just managed to suppress a scream as he looked down into the murky water. Although he didn't believe the stories about water snakes, he wasn't taking any chances.

By the time he'd discovered it was nothing more dangerous than a tuft of rice, the cyclist had passed them and the noise of his ancient machine was fading away into the night.

'Come on, we've lost time,' his father whispered into Lee's ear as soon as he was certain the man was out of earshot, 'If we're late they'll leave without us.'

They swiftly made their way to the end of the paddy. As they climbed the bank they disturbed a small flock of ducks, which protested noisily.

All the sounds Lee heard were familiar but now his ears were hunting for danger in everything and that gave them all a twisted eerie quality. As he squelched along, his eyes searched the gnarled trees whose shadows intertwined, confusing the real with the unreal. They were skirting a swamp that lay between them and the open water beyond, which gave the night birds' calls a deep and mysterious echo.

Breathless, shivering as the night air clung to their damp jeans, Lee and his father caught up with the rest of the family in a clearing on the river bank. They were waiting outside an old hut made of roughly-cut palm planks, whose neglected thatch had been dragged into tufts and holes by countless birds who roosted amongst it.

'I don't like it here,' Tam complained, 'and I want to go home.'

Grandfather silenced her by putting his finger to his lips, and indicated everyone should follow him up the crumbling wooden steps into the decaying hut. They had reached the rendezvous.

In the darkness Lee found a place to squat on the

dank earth floor, he wished he could see more of his fellow passengers. He had to be content to listen to the occasional clearing of a throat or the murmur of a child without even knowing how many others there were.

In these dismal surroundings they sat for nearly an hour. The smaller children grew restive, a baby began to cry until it was suckled, and Lee began to wonder if the whole thing had been called off. Perhaps their boat had already been captured and the soldiers were even now making their way to the hut to round up the passengers.

Apart from the noises inside the hut, the only other sounds came from the soft lapping of the water and the birds who scrabbled amongst the thatch.

Lee almost jumped out of his skin as the hut door suddenly swung open and the figure of a tall, lean man stood silhouetted against the sky. Not a word was spoken but everyone got up, collected their few belongings and shuffled out stiffly.

Anchored some distance from the shore because of the shallow waters of the Mekong Delta, Lee could just make out the low, curved shape of a fishing boat with its small engine-house and short thin mast. As people began to wade out to it in a long line he counted thirty-four, thirty-five including a baby in a shawl on its mother's back. Lee couldn't see how they could all fit into a boat barely nine metres long and only two across at its widest point.

As the first people began slowly to clamber aboard the boat others waited patiently for their turn, waist deep in water. Some had children on their backs, others clutched bundles of food and personal possessions.

The further he got from the shore, the more difficult it was to make each step as the water tried to sweep his feet from under him. Father was carrying Tam but Lee was determined to get to the boat by his own efforts even if he was chest high in water and liable to be swept away by the current.

As the boat gradually began to fill up Lee worried that as they had been the last family to arrive, they would be turned away, but there seemed to be no halt to the number of people and belongings being hoisted on board despite the craft riding noticeably lower in the water.

When it finally came to their family's turn hands were held out to help them. Their black bundles were passed up first, then Kim. Grandfather, in spite of his age, was used to clambering in and out of boats like this one and needed no help but father, having gripped the gunwale, left his legs trailing down the side of the boat and had to be hauled in and landed on the deck with an audible, unceremonious bump.

The closer Lee got to the side of the boat the more it seemed to tower up above him. To make it even more difficult, movement on board made it rock back and forth but Lee had seen one of the other boys about his age manage perfectly well and he was determined to do it too. If he could once get a handhold on the gunwale he would be able to use his feet.

Although he made what seemed a big jump not only did his wet clothes weigh him down but the river seemed to be sucking him down too. Before his hands were half a metre up the sun-bleached planks, he was falling back in and as he fell he lost his footing so that his head disappeared under the muddy stuff and he felt himself being swept away by the current.

He came up coughing and spluttering. Meanwhile his mother had climbed aboard. There were only Lee and his grandmother left.

Lee made two more unsuccessful attempts. He began to have visions of the boat setting off without them when father called out from above.

'Let grandmother help you.'

Lee had been wondering how his ageing grandmother was going to manage if he couldn't, when he felt her hands go round his waist and then, as they held him in an iron grip, she hoisted him right up above her head so that he could easily get hold of the sides. Then she pushed the soles of his feet so hard that before he could stop himself, he had somersaulted into the boat and landed in a tangled heap of arms and legs.

By the time he'd sorted himself out and apologised to the people he'd landed on, his grandmother was standing beside him and he never did find out how she'd done it.

Being the last to board, the only space left was just in front of the engine-house and they all squashed in together as best they could. The only dry things they had were the two black bundles. These were stowed away against the planks of the engine-house while Lee found himself pressed against the weather-worn, fishy-smelling side of the boat.

'Keep your heads down below the sides until they tell us it's safe,' grandfather whispered.

Lee found this almost impossible to achieve in the press of knees, elbows and backs. Just before he ducked his head he saw the outline of the man he'd first seen in the hut doorway. This time he was standing squarely, sculling over the stern with a long single oar.

Crouched down as far as he could go, Lee felt the first movements of the boat as she glided out towards the deeper water in the middle of the river. He saw tops of the trees along the bank slip slowly out of sight as the voyage began.

THREE

As the boat nosed its way steadily downstream towards the wider estuary and the open sea beyond, it was noticed by two soldiers who squatted in the trees on the opposite bank.

Idly they wondered why the man used his energy sculling instead of hoisting the sail until they realised how slight the wind was. Then they asked themselves why he didn't use his engine but in the end they dismissed him as another thrifty fisherman, who was paid so little for his catch that he didn't want to waste the kerosene.

What they didn't notice about the boat, considering it was supposed to be going out empty, was how low it rode in the water. But they were farmers' sons from North Vietnam who knew little of boats, were bored with guarding the river, especially at night, and one of them was still tired from his long, bumpy cycle ride from his billet in the next village.

The people who lay crushed in an untidy heap in the boat knew nothing of the soldiers' ignorance. They didn't even know where they were hiding, all they did know was that they would be out there somewhere and they waited for the sound of the first shot which would signal their discovery.

They had all heard tales of refugee boats sunk by patrols, their survivors picked off with rifles or mown down with automatic weapons. Equally, they knew that untold numbers of refugees who evaded the patrols never made it to Hong Kong or Singapore. Some perished in the unpredictable waters of the South China Sea, others at the hands of ruthless pirates.

Lee felt the knot of excitement tightening in his stomach as he lay with his head pressed against his father's bony kneecaps. Trying to find a more comfortable position, he accidentally banged his head against the wooden side of the boat and the noise made heads turn anxiously towards him.

With nothing to watch but grandmother's fingers plucking nervously at the threads in her black trousers and Tam doing cat's cradles with her mother, time seemed to pass so slowly for Lee. It seemed an odd farewell to the country in which he had been born and brought up. He was surprised that he felt no sadness, perhaps it would have been different if they had been leaving their real home in Cholon. That did seem odd, that he would not be returning to their flat. It was like somebody dying, hard to believe that somebody so familiar was no longer part of your life and you felt slightly cheated.

But at least Lee understood now the importance of the holiday with his grandparents. It was the first holiday Lee ever remembered and at the time it seemed to have been decided on very suddenly.

When they left home his mother had seemed very upset but she'd had a great deal to worry about in recent months and Lee had accepted that as the reason. None of the grown-ups had in fact got much pleasure from the holiday but Lee realised now that they must have spent every moment planning this escape.

Grandfather, who no longer had a boat of his own, usually borrowed one to take them down the river and out to sea, but he didn't bother this time, instead he'd given Lee the clasp-knife to ease the disappointment.

Lee suddenly squirmed round to feel for it in the pockets of his jeans but it wasn't there any more. In his hurry he had forgotten it. It must still be lying on the floor beside his mattress. He felt sick with disappointment. He had been so proud of it, with its shiny, black handle and all its blades and gadgets, some of which he'd never had the chance to use, and now it was gone. He felt tears of annoyance welling up in his eyes, especially when he realised that without the knife he had nothing with him that belonged to Vietnam except the clothes he was wearing and a single stick of chewing gum.

The motion of the boat changed. It began to bob and dip a little and he knew they had left the shelter of the estuary and were out in the open sea. He heard people stirring in the stern and the sound of bare feet on wood as the man who'd been sculling made his way, balanced on the gunwale like a circus performer, to the front of the engine-house.

'You can sit up now,' he said, as he climbed up on the cabin-roof and began hoisting the square sail to catch the slight breeze they could feel in the open water. As it rattled up the short mast, Lee caught a faint whiff of mildew.

When the man had made it fast he climbed down and as he passed he added, 'Keep as quiet as you can. Sound travels easily over water and there are often patrol boats out here so be ready to get down again if I say so. We aren't safe yet!'

Everyone tried to stretch their cramped limbs but with so little room it was far from easy without poking someone else. When Lee moved his leg it throbbed with pins and needles.

'Who is he?' Lee asked as he tried to rub some life back into the aching muscles.

'Trinh,' grandfather replied. 'It was his idea to buy this boat and do it up so that we could escape in it.'

'Escape?' Tam echoed, her eyes wide.

'We're leaving Vietnam forever,' her mother said softly.

'Why?'

'Because it isn't a very nice place to live any more,' mother replied.

When Lee remembered how his parents had had to struggle to find the money to buy their meagre rice ration and how rarely they'd had much to put with it when they got it, he thought this was an understatement. He would never forget the six months his father had spent at Tan Hung, one of the New Economic Zones, working to reclaim and replant the land. While he was away they had no money at all and his mother had been forced to take things from the flat and sell them in the market to buy food for the rest of the family. His father had returned tired and ill. His hands, of which he'd always been rather proud and which were unused to handling anything heavier than a document, were calloused and the usually neat nails ripped and broken.

'Where are we going?' Tam asked.

'Over the sea, a long way,' mother replied and obviously didn't want to bother Tam's head with the details but Lee wanted to know the truth and was going to ask grandfather or father the same question at the earliest opportunity.

'Will there be dragons?' Tam asked; at the moment all her favourite stories had dragons in them.

'I wouldn't be a bit surprised,' mother said and laughed at the horrified expression on her little daughter's face. 'But they'll only be paper ones,' she added and Tam relaxed again.

Lee still hadn't got much feeling in his left leg and decided to try and stand to ease it, but as soon as he did the motion of the boat pitched him sideways and he fell against the shoulder of a woman who was sitting next to them nursing a baby.

'I'm sorry,' Lee mumbled, embarrassed by his own clumsiness.

'That's quite all right,' the woman replied with a smile that seemed to light up the whole of her face like a second moon. 'I'm sure worse will happen before this voyage is over. We are the Duong family. I am Hue, this is my husband Minh and these two are my children, Chi and Quan.'

Lee could see his grandfather disapproved of a woman who took quite so much upon herself but mother stepped in briskly and introduced her family before asking the baby's name.

'Phan,' she replied, clutching the small bundle close to her to keep it from the night air. 'He's only three weeks old and too young to travel really,' a small cloud of doubt slipped across her moon face for a moment, 'but when we got this chance to leave we thought there might never be a second one and I expect Phan will be all right.'

'I'm sure he will,' mother said firmly. She got on well with people and managed to give confidence to anyone who lacked it. 'Where are you from?'

'Saigon . . . I mean Ho Chi Minh City. I've never been able to get used to the new name.'

'Nor me. We were close neighbours then, we're from Cholon.'

Soon they were deep in conversation and Tam was busy talking to Chi although she was nearer to Lee's age than Tam's. Father and Kim were more cautious about new relationships and tried to look as if they weren't listening. So did grandfather but grandmother, although she didn't join in, was nodding and smiling at their discussion.

Lee eyed the boy Quan and wondered what sort of companion he was going to make on the journey. As it was difficult to move about in such confined conditions and the Duong family was next to the Nguyens, it was going to be a help if they liked each other. Quan seemed to have a way of jutting his chin out and looking at you slightly sideways that Lee wasn't sure he liked.

'What did you bring with you?' Quan asked him, pushing the chin even further out and narrowing his eyes, daring Lee to lie about it.

'Nothing,' Lee admitted thinking bitterly about the lost knife and then added, by way of excuse, 'we left in rather a hurry.' He wasn't going to admit that he hadn't been told in advance in case Quan had.

'I brought this,' Quan said. He held up a new,

23

sophisticated, powerful-looking transistor radio which glinted in the moonlight like Quan's eyes now he knew he'd scored a point. The chin swung away in disdain.

Lee had to admit that even if he had brought his own radio, it wouldn't have been nearly as impressive as Quan's. Then he fell to wondering what had happened to all his possessions in Cholon.

He remembered things long forgotten. The way the front door squeaked on wet days and the toys he hadn't played with since he was very small, which were stored away in a cupboard. Just knowing they were there, even though he never took them out, had been a kind of comfort but suddenly knowing he would never see them again Lee felt stripped. It was as if by losing his possessions he had lost his identity. Even now somebody else might be handling them. It was a creepy thought, as if it gave that unknown person some kind of power or a hold over him and he didn't like it.

He was about to ask his father what had happened to the flat and everything in it when he saw that he was busy holding on to Tam who was being violently sick over the side.

Typical, Lee thought, and then banged his chin in his attempt to get his head over the side before it was too late.

'Are you all right, Lee?' his mother asked when eventually he hauled his head back up.

Lee nodded, not trusting himself to speak. He was certain he would have been perfectly all right if Tam hadn't started vomiting. His stomach felt as though it was only anchored to his body by rubber bands on either side, which allowed it to swing back and forth. The trouble was that it wouldn't keep time with the boat and kept tipping back while the boat was already plunging forwards, which left it stranded in mid-air like when a lift starts unexpectedly.

When he realised that the boat sides were lined with fellow-sufferers, it made him feel a little better until he

24

noticed the grin of triumph on Quan's face. Lee began to think he wasn't going to like Quan an awful lot, but the thought was wiped from his mind as he grabbed the side of the boat again and retched and retched until long after anything which might have come up had come up. His throat and body ached with pain and effort.

He was still heaving away when he dimly heard Trinh shouting from the stern. 'Get down, everybody!'

Lee looked up and saw, some distance off but coming towards them, red and green navigation lights and knew it must be a naval patrol boat because of its speed.

As the deep-throated thrum of the boat's powerful engines drew closer Lee crouched down still retching and lay huddled in a miserable heap surrounded by the smell of his own bile.

Kim let out a startled cry as the brilliant beam of a searchlight pierced the darkness and swept the fishing boat from stem to stern. By its reflected light Lee could clearly see the haunted look on the faces of the other passengers. It was a sharp contrast to the almost holiday atmosphere which had begun to develop on the boat as it got into the estuary when everybody was busy settling in and introducing themselves.

Lee knew that if the patrol boat got close enough, its men would be bound to see the people crouched down in the fishing-boat. Surrounded by the smell of fish, tar, engine oil and vomit he began to feel hot and dizzy. His body was stiff with fear, aching from seasickness and he felt he might faint at any moment. To keep himself conscious he twisted his neck round so that he could see Trinh standing in the stern holding the tiller. He was blinking in the harsh light but he managed to wave back at the patrol boat as if he hadn't a care in the world.

A Tannoy was switched on aboard the patrol boat and a voice, made harsh and thin by its horn, demanded, 'Where are you bound?'

Trinh shrugged and shouted back. 'Tell me where the fish run and I'll tell you where I'm bound.'

The noise of the patrol boat's idling engines drowned his voice.

'Say again!' barked the hailer.

'Anywhere where there's fish,' Trinh shouted back.

There was a pause. The boats drifted closer to each other.

'Why aren't you showing navigation lights?'

Lee watched as Trinh pretended to look puzzled and leant out over the side as if to see what they said were true.

'They must have blown out,' he apologised with a shrug. 'I'll light them again as soon as you stop rocking me about like this.'

There was another, longer pause. The boats kept drifting closer and Lee, not daring to breathe again, watched as the spotlight dipped and bobbed with the motion of the patrol boat, convinced it would only be seconds before a sailor on its bridge got a glimpse of somebody's back.

Aboard the patrol boat, the captain was wondering if it would be worth while searching this dowdy old fishing-boat for contraband when the radio crackled into life.

Abruptly, without another word being exchanged, the light snapped off and the patrol boat revved its engines speeding off into the dark, leaving the fishing-boat bobbing about like a cork in its vicious wake.

In the darkness which followed the spotlight's glare the passengers began to relax.

'What happened—why did they go away?' Lee asked.

'Perhaps they were called away to something more important,' father suggested.

'But they will have noted the identity number of this boat,' grandfather said quietly. 'Whatever happens we'll *have* to keep going now.'

Lee clutched his sore stomach. He wondered if the prospect of weeks at sea was quite the adventure he'd expected.

'I want to go home,' Tam said in a very small voice and although Lee scowled at her he knew that most of the people on board wished that that was possible too.

FOUR

Lee slept fitfully that first night. His stomach ached and his head and eyes felt swollen. Besides there wasn't room to lie down. Mother, father, Tam and Kim slept upright all huddled together but Lee didn't think that was right for a twelve-year-old-boy and tried to sleep with his back against the side of the boat.

When he woke up, which was every half hour or so, the night was punctuated by the slop, slop of the sea, the sobs of children and the moans of the older women who dreamt of home. When he did drift into sleep he constantly dreamt of falling down the stair-well outside their Cholon flat.

He was wide awake when the sun rose out of the mist as a pale pink disc and he knelt up to look over the side at the view. There was nothing but sea on every side. Whenever Lee had spent the day with grandfather there had always been other boats, birds and the coastline to watch, but here there was nothing to see except the sun shrivelling up the morning mist to reveal even more sea.

Grandfather was the next to wake. Almost before the old man had had time to stretch, Lee was plying him with questions.

'Where are we heading?'

'Hong Kong, if the wind will let us.'

Lee knew very little about Hong Kong apart from pictures he'd seen of skyscrapers and crowded streets. 'How long will it take us to get there?'

'At least two weeks.'

To Lee a fortnight sounded a very long time to be cramped up in an old boat, seasick and unable to sleep.

'And what if the wind won't let us go to Hong Kong?' he asked.

'Then we'll have to go somewhere else.'

The old man coughed deeply. Then, without rising, he spat lustily in a vast curved arc so that it glinted in the sun before landing in the sea. This was a talent Lee greatly coveted and practised for hours in vain. His father totally disapproved although he would never have dreamt of saying so.

Lee glanced up at the sagging sail with its patches of brown mildew edged with salt stains and couldn't believe that it would ever get them to Hong Kong or anywhere else. As the sun had climbed higher in the sky, the wind had died away until the sail was hardly troubled by it all but occasionally flapped limply against the mast.

'Why don't we use the engine?' Lee asked.

'Because we only have a very limited supply of fuel and we can only use it if we really have to. Mind you,' he said, shading his eyes against the sun and looking at the cloudless sky, 'if we're to make any headway today I think that moment's arrived.'

Indeed as he spoke Trinh, who had been at the helm all night, padded along the gunwale and swung himself down into the engine-house.

Lee heard the engine give a cough. Grandfather looked anxious. There were several more coughs each one followed by silence and the expression on grandfather's face grew more and more serious each time. Eventually the engine burst into an uncertain life but it continued to misfire. Grandfather relaxed and climbed up on to the engine-house roof to let the tattered sail rattle down the mast as the boat began to move more forcefully through the water.

The vibration, the engine's irregular rhythm together with the oily fumes which drifted up from it soon woke those passengers still asleep. Most still suffered from seasickness. They rubbed their eyes, stretched their limbs, looking exhausted after just one night and Lee couldn't help wondering how they would all last a fortnight of this.

Only grandfather, Trinh, and the little baby Phan, who was being breastfed anyway, managed breakfast.

'Why isn't the baby sick like the rest of us?' Lee wanted to know.

'Because he's only just spent nine months floating about in his mother's stomach,' Lee's mother explained. 'To the baby constant movement like this seems perfectly natural, which is why you used to like being in a shawl on my back.'

'I did too, didn't I?' Tam murmured from where she was curled up in her mother's lap. She looked pale and didn't bother to open her eyes to speak, but, ill as she was, refused to be left out of the conversation for long.

'Yes, you did,' mother replied and stroked the hair back off her forehead.

'You still do,' Lee retorted. 'You had to be carried to the boat.'

'Only because it was dark and there might have been dragons,' Tam sat up to defend herself.

'Dragons!'

'There might . . .'

Tam would have said more but having sat up too quickly, had to rush to the side to be sick. Father held her head.

'Lee!' mother said quietly. 'Leave the poor girl alone, you can see she isn't well.'

'I'll go and see what grandfather's doing,' Lee suggested.

'Don't make a nuisance of yourself,' father said, looking over his shoulder from helping Tam. 'There isn't much room to move about so you'll have to get used to sitting still while we're on the boat.'

Grandfather was preparing lines for fishing, baiting them with the remains of his breakfast noodles.

'Can I help?' Lee asked.

Grandfather nodded. 'I'll show you how it's done and then you can do it next time.'

Lee watched the nimble fingers baiting the hooks and

then saw the lines trailing alongside the boat in the water. From this vantage point on top of the engine-house Lee was able to get his first good look at the whole boat by daylight. His guess of nine metres overall length was about right and crammed with people she looked even smaller. The boat's age could best be judged by the number of different coloured coats of paint peeling off the engine-house, but also by the sun-bleached, weather-worn planks of the boat itself. When new she must have been a handsome boat but it was obvious that she had been cobbled together for years to keep her afloat at all.

Lee looked anxiously at the small woven coracle, strapped to the engine-house by a length of frayed rope and wondered how many people it could hold if this old boat sprang a leak.

'I've got a bite,' grandfather said under his breath and proceeded to haul out a fat silvery fish. He slapped it down on the roof, took out a murderous looking knife and began to gut it.

'You said you wanted to bait the hooks,' grandfather said, passing him the line, 'we can use the innards for that.'

Lee took one look at his grandfather's scale-slimy hands and at the squishy bits on the engine roof, shook his head quickly and left, hoping that he'd make it to the side and not be sick on the deck.

It was midday before most people were able to take more than water. A spirit stove was rigged up on the engine-house roof and those who felt stronger produced bowls and chopsticks to eat a little rice. Several people, like Lee, thought they would like to try some but couldn't keep it down.

The sun was very hot and grandfather found a spare sail which they could rig up to create a little shade as there wasn't the slightest puff of wind. Lee and Kim crawled beneath it and slept for over an hour more from exhaustion than anything else.

When Lee woke he noticed grandfather was missing and asked where he was.

'Steering the boat while Trinh gets some sleep,' his father replied.

'Can I go and help him?'

'Remember what I said about getting used to sitting still?'

'Yes, but I'd like to help. Grandfather used to let me steer sometimes.'

'Go carefully. Remember you haven't got your sea-legs properly yet. I should go barefoot like Trinh and grandfather while you're on the boat.'

Lee took off his shoes and passed them to his mother who stowed them away in one of the black bundles which seemed to serve as wardrobe, pantry and everything else.

The warning his father had given him about his sea-legs seemed silly until Lee tried to walk along the narrow planks between the engine-house and the side of the boat. He found it very difficult to keep his balance and was almost pitched into the sea twice before he reached his grandfather's side in the stern.

Although grandfather nodded to acknowledge Lee's arrival he didn't speak. He was a very quiet man, used to long periods at sea alone. Lee thought he often seemed ill at ease, even slightly clumsy on land, but the moment he boarded a boat he was always totally at home.

Lee had particularly noticed this in the relationship between his father and grandfather. Naturally grandfather was the head of the family and made all the important decisions but grandfather always seemed far happier when the questions concerned the world he knew and understood rather than the sophisticated world in which father lived.

'What time is it?' the old man asked at last, his hand resting lightly on the thin metal tiller.

Lee looked at his digital watch. 'Fifteen hundred hours.'

'Huh?' the old man grunted and Lee remembered he refused to have anything to do with the twenty-four-hour clock.

'Three o'clock, grandfather,' he translated. 'Why do you need to know?'

'We navigate by the sun during the day and the stars at night,' grandfather explained, his eyes never leaving the horizon.

'What happens if the sun and stars are covered by clouds? Wouldn't it be safer to use charts and a compass?'

'It would, if we had such things. But fishermen who are really going out to fish don't use compasses. Even if you could, trying to buy one would attract the attention of the authorities and you certainly wouldn't be able to buy the charts we would need without telling everybody what we were about to do.'

'But without a chart how do you know where we will end up?'

'But we have got a map,' the old man said and reached down behind his feet to pull out a transparent plastic folder which he handed to Lee.

It was a single page which had been torn out of an old school atlas. The scale was very small. Vietnam showed only as a short thin sliver on a map which ranged from the vast mass of China in the north to the curving line of islands which make up Indonesia in the south. In the very top right-hand corner was a tiny dot marked Hong Kong. It seemed so small and far away that Lee couldn't believe they would ever be able to find it.

Then he frowned. 'Where is the sun at three o'clock?' he asked.

'In the south-west.'

'But, grandfather,' Lee said carefully not wishing to criticise the old man, 'Hong Kong is north-east of Vietnam according to this map but my shadow is falling out of the left side of the boat.'

The old man nodded patiently, secretly pleased that

Lee had worked that out for himself. He'd always believed that the family should have stuck to the sea and was bitterly disappointed that neither of his sons had followed in his footsteps.

'Which means that we are heading east,' Grandfather nodded again. 'But we want to be clear of Vietnamese waters as soon as possible so that we don't run the risk of being stopped by any more patrol boats, like the one we met last night. Tomorrow we'll head towards the north but for today we go east. Now that you know where to keep your shadow, you can take the tiller.' Grandfather shifted to make room for him.

Although Lee had often steered boats with grandfather in the past, that had been in the calm inshore waters and he was surprised and excited, even a little frightened, as he held the tiller to feel for the first time the powerful strength of the open sea. The constant pull of water on the rudder made it clear who was really master out here and Lee felt a sense of menace in this alien environment. In that moment, too, he also knew why it had fascinated grandfather all his life and why his father, who preferred a predictable, orderly existence containing problems which only existed in the mind, would never have been happy as a fisherman. It made his decision to escape, with all the tangible problems that involved, all the more surprising.

'Look where you're going,' grandfather said sharply almost as if Lee was about to bump into something.

Lee glanced at his shadow and was surprised to see it astern of the boat. He corrected the course but was astonished that grandfather even knew he was off course in the first place. He had never once taken his eyes off the horizon but where Lee saw only a vast expanse of sea grandfather appeared to see troughs and hollows as if it were land. Either that or he had an inbuilt compass, a sixth sense that told him where to go!

'Why didn't my uncle come with us?' Lee asked and wished he hadn't when he saw his grandfather's jaw set more firmly, pushing out the cheekbones, making the flesh seem thinner.

'Because there wasn't enough money,' he explained quietly. 'Trinh had to buy the boat, as you know, and it was very expensive although it's so old. After that repairs were needed and most of the materials had to be bought on the black market which made them very dear. So all the people on board bought their passages from Trinh to pay for all that, on top of which food had to be provided and enough money left over to buy things we might need on the way.' He paused for a moment and sighed deeply. 'When the cost was worked out we realised we hadn't enough money between us in the family and so your uncle, Loc, decided that he would lend us his share and stay behind.'

'Didn't he want to come?'

'Very much but he said that as he wasn't married and had no children it was more important that we should all go and one day he would follow and join us when we are settled in our new home. It was a very generous thing that he did.'

'It was,' Lee agreed. 'Are you glad you are leaving Vietnam?'

Grandfather considered this carefully before he answered. 'No, but these are not good times for people like us, who are of Chinese origin, to live in Vietnam.'

'But Chinese people have lived in Vietnam for thousands of years,' Lee protested.

'Yes and many have grown fat, especially while first the French and later the Americans ran Vietnam. But since the war the new government has used us as the scapegoats for everything that has gone wrong. The Chinese invasion of North Vietnam was all the excuse they needed to take our money, our land and our jobs away from us. Now they only offer us jobs for which we are unsuited, pay us low wages and leave us at the end of the queue when the rice rations are handed out.'

'It's so unfair,' declared Lee bitterly.

'Maybe,' grandfather nodded, 'but from war there are few winners and many losers.'

'I suppose with father working for the South Vietnamese government that only made things worse because it was like working for the Americans but that didn't mean you had to leave too.'

'No, I could have lived out what is left of my life in Vietnam but we wouldn't like to be separated from the rest of the family and we know there is no future for you young ones so we decided to make the journey with you. Apart from which I am a fisherman. I know the ways of the sea and I thought I could see you safely to your new home.'

'We may find a new home but I will always think of myself as Vietnamese not Chinese.'

'That's good,' grandfather smiled, 'but right now if you are to find that new home you'd better pay more attention to your steering, you're letting us drift again.'

'My arms are aching,' Lee admitted.

'The seasickness has made you weak. Give me the tiller and you shall steer again when you are stronger.'

'I don't think I'll ever stop being sick completely,' Lee said ruefully.

'The first two days are always the worst. Very few people never stop. By tomorrow, you'll see, you'll be eating again and it's always better to be sick on a full stomach than an empty one.'

The thought of food was enough to make Lee feel queasy and he got up to leave.

'Before you go,' grandfather said, 'I've got something of yours.'

In the hard-skinned palm of grandfather's hand lay the shiny, black clasp-knife Lee thought he would never see again.

Lee was still clutching the knife when he rejoined the family to find Tam in tears. It seemed that she, too, had been asking questions but it was one particular aspect which had upset her.

'What about my dolls?' she sobbed.

'We had to leave everything,' mother said, 'otherwise people would have got suspicious and reported us to the authorities.'

'But I want them!'

'Tam,' father said, trying to soothe her, 'don't cry.'

In a sudden burst of generosity, partly because he felt guilty now that he had his beloved knife back, Lee offered to buy her a new doll. 'The biggest doll you've ever seen.'

'But I want my old ones,' Tam declared but there was a gap in her tears as she considered his offer. 'One with hair you can wash and set?'

'If you like,' Lee said beginning to wonder what his impetuous offer was likely to cost but at least Tam had calmed down. He turned to father. 'What's happened about the flat?'

'Loc has the keys and if nothing is heard of us for a week he'll assume we've escaped and hand the keys back to the landlord.'

'Grandfather says we're going to Hong Kong. Where will we live when we get there?'

'In a refugee camp.'

'For the rest of our lives?' Kim asked. She looked horrified.

'Only until we can find a country which will take us. Then we'll probably go and live in America. Because I worked for them in Vietnam they'll probably take us. After all that was the main reason I lost my job. The new Vietnamese don't trust the ethnic Chinese anyway but those who worked for the Americans they like least of all.'

Apart from going to the stern to collect water from the white plastic bottles, covered by a wet cloth to keep them cool and reasonably fresh, few people moved for the rest of the day. Most of them struggled to cope with seasickness and uncertainty of what lay ahead.

To Lee, as everyone else, everything seemed upside

37

down. Yesterday he'd expected to return after the holiday to the familiar friends, relatives and streets in Cholon. Now his whole life was contained in this rickety boat bobbing about on the South China Sea. His parents, on whom he'd always been able to rely in the past, knew little more than he did about the future and he was weak from hunger although he still couldn't keep food down.

That evening as the sun set it seemed to be bleeding into the sea and Lee, in spite of the physical closeness of his family, felt an awful sense of loneliness. When he eventually fell asleep he clutched his clasp-knife so hard his knuckles went white.

FIVE

'We're using too much drinking water too quickly,' Trinh announced.

Everyone was beginning to feel a little better, even Lee had managed some rice soup for breakfast, and a meeting was in progress to organise life on board. While another man took the helm, Trinh and grandfather sat cross-legged on the cabin-roof so that they could see everybody.

'We're going to have to ration the water otherwise our supply will run out long before we reach land,' Trinh continued, turning to grandfather for support. Although it was Trinh's boat he seemed constantly to defer to grandfather, not only because he was the oldest aboard but also because of his great experience.

Grandfather nodded. 'I suggest one rice-bowl of water each a day until we see how things go. Hung, would you take charge of the water?' A tough-looking man with a very serious face nodded slowly and Lee couldn't help thinking it would be easier to get blood out of a stone than extra water out of that man.

'The other thing,' Trinh went on, 'is cooking. On a wooden boat like this it's going to be very dangerous if every family has a stove to cook on. I think we should organise a kitchen to cook for everybody.'

This caused a good deal of argument. Many people thought they had brought more food than the rest and didn't see why they should share their expensive rations. In the end, to save fuel and for safety, it was agreed that the rice should be cooked communally but individual families would prepare and cook whatever they wanted with it.

'But when the weather is suitable all cooking will be done up here on the cabin-roof,' grandfather said firmly.

39

'I've got part of an old sail we can rig up as a shelter,' Trinh offered.

Then they drew up rotas not only for cooking the rice but for watches, night and day, and for cleaning orderlies.

'With people eating all over the boat it would be very easy to turn the place into a pigsty and that's when accidents start happening,' Trinh warned them.

'It would be very difficult to treat somebody with a broken leg out here!' Grandfather agreed. 'We haven't a doctor with us but Lan is a trained nurse. I suggest you would all be far safer if you walked barefoot like Trinh and me.'

Lee noticed that those people who had not already removed their shoes did so except for the man sitting next to the nurse, Lan. He continued to wear his stiff expensive leather shoes as if he thought somebody might steal them should he leave them anywhere.

'While we're on the subject of illness,' Lan said, 'I've managed to get hold of some antibiotics, penicillin and so on, so if anybody feels ill please come and tell me straight away. Cramped together like this, illness could spread like wildfire and I'd rather tackle something in the early stages sooner than face an epidemic.'

'Which brings us to personal cleanliness,' Trinh said. 'We're arranging a bucket lavatory in the engine-house. Each person is responsible for washing it out after use. For that you must use seawater and the same goes for washing, including clothing. There are plenty of plastic buckets stowed away in the prow and the stern.'

'We shall also need help with running the boat,' grandfather pointed out. 'At the moment we are the only two capable of handling her without assistance and that is obviously not a good thing in case anything should happen to one of us. So we'll be arranging to teach all the men on board in turn.'

'I'd also like help with the engine. An engineer, who said he was coming with us, backed out at the last moment,' Trinh said. 'I've done the best I could with the engine but I'd feel a good deal happier if somebody else could have a look at it.'

He looked round expectantly but nobody volunteered. Lee was dying to offer his help but he knew only too well how much his father disapproved of his interest in engines of any kind, and this didn't seem to be the moment to confess that back in Cholon he'd been spending most Saturdays helping at the local garage to get broken-down vehicles back on the road.

It seemed to be a family characteristic that the Nguyen sons did not want to follow the fathers' professions. Loc had got the nearest, he sold fish in his shop in Cholon!

So Trinh did not get the help he was looking for and the meeting broke up to allow everyone to go about their own business, or at least those whose names did not appear on the rotas which came into effect straight away as Quan discovered.

'Did you know,' he asked Lee, 'that we're on watch together tonight? I bet you fall asleep!' He jutted his chin out again.

'I bet I don't,' Lee retorted angrily.

'What do you bet?'

'My knife against your radio,' said Lee willing to sacrifice his proudest possession to put down the boastful Quan.

'I've got a knife twice as good as that in Saigon,' Quan said scornfully.

'Well, you'll never see it again now,' Lee grinned. 'So if you're so sure why not make the bet?'

'But my radio's worth a hundred times more than what your knife's worth.'

'The only reason you won't bet is because you know you're going to lose.' Lee thought he'd got Quan where he wanted him now.

'The reason I won't take the bet,' said Quan, jutting his chin so high that it was all Lee could see of his face, 'is because if I win, I win nothing.'

And with that he turned away, closing the discussion and leaving Lee smarting, determined to catch Quan out at the earliest opportunity.

Now that most people had recovered from seasickness they quickly learned that for those not involved in the four-hour duty rotas, the next enemy was going to be boredom. Although the meeting had occupied an hour after breakfast, it seemed a long time to the midday meal with very little to do.

The women soon got through their chores of washing and mending and the men played cards or talked. The children longed for some exercise but, on a boat so full that it was difficult to find a space to sit, there was little chance of that.

'We could always go for a swim,' Kim said when Tam said she was sick of sitting still. 'The one thing we aren't short of is water!'

But nobody on board would have fancied the idea even if the boat had been stationary in a flat calm. Whilst it would have been a wonderful way to exercise and cleanse themselves at the same time, even after two nights and a morning at sea their view of it had changed. They no longer saw it as picturesque or friendly and they were not yet in the position of Trinh and grandfather who worked alongside it as a colleague to be treated with great respect. The majority viewed it with slight fear as something to be endured.

'You could always do exercises where you sit,' Lan suggested brightly and promptly demonstrated a whole series of arm, head and leg movements designed to ease stiffness.

Lee rapidly lost interest and played cards with Tam until she started cheating because she wasn't winning. Several people had brought radios with them to relieve the boredom, but the further they got from land the weaker the signals were until only Quan's more powerful one could be used to received news broadcasts and the vital weather forecasts from the Voice of Vietnam. But Quan also listened to music on some of the foreign stations until his father suggested this wasn't a good idea.

'You ought to save the batteries,' he said, 'now that your set is the only one that can get the weather forecasts. After all, it could save our lives if there was a typhoon warning for the area.'

In the silence which followed after the radio was shut off, Lee started worrying about something else that had secretly bothered him from the moment he'd heard they were leaving.

An adventure, in theory, sounded all very well, although this voyage so far showed little sign of being one, but if there were going to be typhoons, how brave would he be in the face of real danger?

It was obvious Quan, who was fast becoming his arch-rival, would stick out his chin to face anything and although Lee knew he could run along the top of a high wall or try to be last across the road in front of an advancing lorry with his schoolfriends, those were just stupid games you played as dares. This was very real. He had often heard the boat people described as heroes and Lee's version of a hero included fighter pilots, explorers and mountaineers. He couldn't see himself matching up to their examples and yet he was determined not to be outdone by Quan!

The silence, which Lee had filled with his own disturbing thoughts, was broken by the voice of a girl singing. He turned and discovered it was Chi who was helping her mother with the washing. She sang some of the old songs they all knew from home and slowly more and more people joined in too. Some of the older people had tears in their eyes, especially when they sang one called 'Tomorrow we'll be back'.

Knowing that he was to go on watch at midnight Lee hadn't expected to sleep but he was woken by Hung, who'd had the earlier watch, shaking him roughly by

43

the shoulder before he moved on to wake Quan.

His eyes still heavy with sleep Lee folded up his blanket and felt the cool night air against his skin.

'I've seen nothing all night,' Hung said wearily before he left them to make his way back to his own family. 'There's a bit of wind so Trinh's stopped the engine and raised the sail.'

After Hung had left them Quan asked, 'Do you want to be on the cabin or in the bow?'

The idea was that the person in the bow could shout to the cabin and the second person could relay the message to the helmsman, who himself kept watch from the stern. It was Trinh that night. With the sail up, there was no doubt about it, the people in the stern and on the cabin would have a very limited view. Lee who would normally have been polite and let the other person choose didn't because it was Quan, and opted for the bow.

Lee carefully picked his way amongst the sleeping people to his place in the bow and settled down. He had heard people complaining during the day that there was little to see but for the occasional seabird or lump of flotsam and the most exciting thing they had to look out for was shallow water. But now there was nothing at all surrounded by the black velvet of the night except the odd star. In these circumstances it was very difficult to manage total concentration and more difficult to avoid his imagination taking over.

Several times Lee had almost called out to Quan that he had seen something only to discover, just in time, that when he blinked the object vanished.

After what seemed like hours of fruitless watching, with nothing to listen to but the snores of one of the sleepers and the water creaming beneath the boat, Lee looked at the luminous figures on his watch to see how much of the four-hour watch was still left. He was shocked to discover only half-an-hour had passed.

He rested his chin on the smooth wood of the side of

the boat. Traces of mist drifted by, lit only by the red and green oil-burning navigation light on either side of the boat. He discovered he couldn't even see the sail, let alone Quan, through the darkness, just the small light which swung from the top of the mast in time with the motion of the boat.

He was delighted when he realised the motion of the boat no longer made him feel the least bit sick but grew worried when he found it starting to rock him to sleep.

His eyelids grew heavy and began to droop. He rubbed his face with his hands and sat up to try and keep himself awake but it was no use. Try as he might, the gentle motion of the boat and the hypnotic sound of the water passing easily under the boat took Lee off into a sound sleep.

He awoke with a violent start when his head slipped off the side of the boat. He looked at his watch and was ashamed to discover that he'd been asleep for nearly an hour. He glanced round to see if anybody had noticed but it was too dark to tell. He rubbed his arms with his hands to get some warmth back into them and looked out to sea. The mist was thicker than before.

Then he stopped still to listen. He thought he could hear a noise some distance off. It was hard to tell because of the noises closer to hand and he was just about to dismiss it as more imagination when he heard it again, a little closer this time.

He cupped his ears in his hands to try and hear more clearly and to cut out the snores and grunts of the sleepers. Quite definitely there was something out there, it sounded like a boat but not like the patrol boat's engines. These were deeper and steadier. But from which direction was it coming? He had to know.

He peered hard into the mist to try and locate the sound but could see nothing. Then suddenly he caught sight of some lights. They were higher than he'd expected but coming straight towards him.

'Quan! Quan!' Lee shouted as hard as he could.

'There's a boat coming straight at us.'

There was no answer from Quan.

'Quan!' he shouted again.

People around him began to stir.

'What is it?' Trinh called to him from the stern where the sail obscured his view of the boat that was bearing down on them.

'There's a ship coming straight for us!'

'Quan,' Trinh shouted, 'start the engine!'

At the same moment he pushed the tiller hard over but with only a slight wind the boat's movement was sluggish. Certainly too slow to get them out of the ship's path.

'Lee,' Trinh called again. 'Quan must have fallen asleep. Get the engine started before that damn cargo boat runs us down!'

Lee scrambled through the waking people as best he could with the sound of the ship's huge engines drumming in his ears. Just short of the engine-house he stepped on something soft, lost his balance and went crashing on to the deck but he scrambled to his feet again. A split second before he swung himself down into the engine-cabin, Lee caught a brief glimpse of Quan, still curled up asleep on the roof.

As Lee fumbled round in the dark to find the starting-handle he heard people shouting at the ship as if they thought it might alter its course if someone heard them above the blanketing noise of its engines. By now he could feel vibrations from its massive engines through the soles of his feet.

He found the starting-handle and with his other hand felt round the greasy engine for the fuel tap. He switched on the tap and then traced the fuel-pipe round to the carburettor. Never having seen this engine close to, his misspent Saturday mornings at the garage stood him in good stead now as he had no light and had to rely totally on his knowledge and sense of touch.

His hand shook a little as he pushed the button on top

46

of the carburettor and felt the cold kerosene run over his fingers from the hole in the side. She was primed, but would she start?

As Lee gripped the starting-handle, he remembered the problems Trinh, who was much stronger than he, had had. He swung the handle. The engine coughed. His second swing was longer and stronger, so were the coughs but she still wouldn't fire.

'Come out and let me get to it!' Hung shouted from the doorway.

But Lee, having let everyone down by falling asleep, was determined that he would be the one to start the engine. He gave it a final swing. He swung it so hard and so fast that the handle flew out of its socket. He fell backwards against the full cans of kerosene but as he fell he heard the engine cough and falter before it burst into an uncertain but continuous life. But was it already too late?

As he climbed back up on deck he noticed that Quan was awake now and was sitting watching, ashen-faced, with the useless sail flapping about his ears as the ship, only a few metres away, towered above them like a skyscraper.

The people on the fishing-boat still screamed but the lights on the deck and the bridge showed no sign of anyone. Probably illegally left on automatic pilot, it moved through the water like a relentless ghost.

Trinh knew there were two main dangers. First, as the bow passed they would be sucked towards the ship and might be smashed against its steel side. Second, even if they avoided that fate, the stern wave might swamp them.

The fishing-boat's puny engine was no match for the cargo boat but there was still time to get them out of its immediate path.

'Hold hard!' he yelled.

The great pointed prow of the cargo boat slipped by them. Trinh felt a slight pull which wasn't enough to do any damage but during the time it took for the ship to pass them, the fishing-boat seemed to make almost no headway so that when the stern wave hit them it tipped the little boat on end.

People screamed. They were hurled about with their possessions in the dark. A huge wave of water crashed in on top of them before the boat had righted itself. The water hit Lee with the force of a wall, knocking him off his feet. For an instant he wondered if he would be swept overboard, and he knew that in the dark there would be little hope of finding anyone. The water filled his eyes, ears and nose leaving him gasping for breath but swallowing salt water instead of air until he choked. Then the water dropped him with a crash on to the wood of the deck leaving him stunned and bruised.

When Lee picked himself up he discovered Quan, who had fallen off the roof when the boat tilted so violently, sitting next to him. No words were exchanged. Quan was not only bedraggled but suffering from a severe loss of face. His chin no longer jutted but was sunk deep into his soaking-wet chest.

Grandfather, equally wet but grinning with pride, clapped Lee heartily on the shoulder. 'You managed to start the brute, good boy!'

'Perhaps it's as well he understands engines after all,' his mother said with a smile and a glance at her husband. Father didn't reply but his quiet smile told Lee that although he would never enjoy the thought of Lee as an engineer he was pleased about what Lee had done to save the boat.

'You needn't have trodden on me though,' Kim said holding up her arm to show him an ugly bruise.

'I'm sorry.'

While everyone tried to sort out themselves and their soaking-wet belongings Lee turned away. He'd found their praise embarrassing because he didn't believe he truly deserved it. As he watched the lights of the cargo ship being swallowed up again by the mist he thought how lucky he'd been that he had woken before Quan.

SIX

'I hate fish!' Tam announced loudly.

The huge wave that had followed the near collision with the cargo boat had not only soaked the occupants but had also spoilt much of their dwindling fresh food. They had already been running short of pork and chicken but now what little fruit, leaf vegetables and eggs had not gone putrid in the unrelenting heat had been ruined by the sea-water. Even some of their essential rice was damaged. Consequently fishing was no longer a pastime but had become a vital necessity.

'But you were always asking for fish at grandmother's,' her mother said soothingly.

'But it's different now,' Tam replied.

Lee had to admit that it was beginning to taste a little like salted rubber but he knew there was little point in protest and tried hard to think of something else, anything else, while he ate it.

Even the idea of eating outside had lost its attraction now it happened every day, and since there was little enough food for meals there was nothing left for snacks which they were all used to at home. Lee longed for some of the fried snacks he used to buy from the Cholon streetsellers on the way home from school.

What Lee couldn't understand was why they had to preserve fish when it was so easy to catch them.

'Because if we had storms there would be no fish at all,' grandfather explained.

All the men on board fished with varying degrees of success. Many gambled on their own prowess and lost large sums of money.

'That's the trouble with the Chinese,' grandfather said shaking his head, 'they gamble on anything. Two flies going up a wall would do. It's been the making and the breaking of the Chinese!'

Although he wouldn't join in on the gambling he was happy to show the winners successful ways of preserving their fish, if not their winnings.

For both methods the head, tail, and backbone were removed. In the first the fillets were then laid between pieces of sailcloth which were sprinkled with sea-water from time to time. The bundle was kept in the shade and the evaporating water, with the salt deposits left behind, would keep the fish in reasonable condition for a few days.

But for long-term preservation drying was better. For this each day the fillets were hung out to dry like washing on a line and they were taken down to avoid mildew in the humid nights. Depending on the thickness this could take hours, days or weeks but when properly dried and bound tightly in cloth to exclude air, the fish would keep for a long time.

Despite all the hard work or perhaps because of it, in such cramped conditions, squabbles broke out. Usually they were over the silliest things and the children would watch with amazement as grown-ups squabbled over everything from who snored loudest to who had the most drying space for clothes.

The worst quarrels were over water and food. Some people claimed that others were getting more than their fair share of water because Hung had favourites, which was nonsense of course.

Having agreed to rice being cooked communally first of all, there was trouble about people who had lost their rice when the boat was swamped. After bitter discussion that was solved by pooling all the rice on board. Then arguments broke out, mainly among those who had reluctantly handed over their stores, over who was served first. It seemed that some were always at the head of the queue while others always had to wait.

It was suggested they should queue in alphabetical order but nobody could agree whether this should be in order of family names or first names. Family names would be complicated as there are few in Vietnam and many unrelated people shared the same name, but first names would mean young children being separated from their parents.

In the end they decided to keep muddling along as before but it often led to secret mistrust which was only a symptom of the main problem, their struggle for survival in this foreign environment with such cramped and awful conditions.

Several people had already developed diarrhoea because of the limited diet and, in spite of every attempt to prevent it, the stench was building up.

Lee's own personal irritation was salt. It seemed to get everywhere. Not only into the food but in his clothes, his eyebrows and his hair. It crusted his nostrils whenever he breathed and coated his tongue when he licked his lips.

Every movement, no matter how slight, brought his skin grating against the grains which had dried in his clothes after washing, and they rubbed his skin raw as surely as if they'd been made of sandpaper.

He had to use salt water to clean his teeth. There was no need for toothpaste, it was abrasive enough without and left him with a raging thirst he could not satisfy because water was rationed.

Sores were starting to form on his face and arms partially from the salt but also from the lack of fresh vegetables in his diet. It was the same for everyone and Lee admitted he was lucky. Because there were seven in his family he got water to drink seven times a day. This didn't mean he got any more, just more frequently.

At regular intervals each person in the family would collect their rice bowl of water and share it with the others, handing it round for each person to take a sip. Even now, when the water was getting stale and starting to be tainted by the plastic containers, this moment when the precious drops of salt-free liquid cleared the mouth just for a few seconds was one of the best. The only trouble was it didn't last long enough and left you thirstier than before.

Then something happened which took all their minds off their problems.

Minh was on watch on the engine-house roof. He'd been sitting cross-legged helping grandfather mend the ragged sail when he looked up and saw a boat, similar to their own, a short distance off and heading towards them.

Dropping his work he stood up and shouted. 'Look! there's a boat.'

Everyone stood up and started shouting, cheering and waving. It was the first boat they'd seen of any description since the cargo vessel.

Lee viewed it with mixed feelings. Out there with nothing to see but the horizon all around he had begun to believe they were the only people still alive in the whole world. He had found this thought a little frightening but now couldn't help resenting these people. It was as if they were intruding into his private and personal world.

He had had a similar feeling once in hospital. When he was recovering he wanted to get out of the hospital as quickly as he could and see his friends again but when they came to visit him, he slightly wished they hadn't and was relieved to get back to the hospital routine after they'd gone.

But this was soon forgotten in the hubbub of shouts and laughter which drifted across the water between the two boats as they drew closer together.

'How many are you?' Trinh shouted, above the noise of the engines.

'Forty-five,' their helmsman called back.

The boat was the same size as theirs and Lee could see that amongst the steaming cook pots and brightly coloured washing, which hung limp in the windless air, how much more crowded it was.

'Where are you from?' Trinh asked.

'Dong Hoi.'

'But that's in the north,' Lee said to his father.

'People are leaving from all over Vietnam, not just the south,' his father replied.

When the boats were very close a boy tossed a brightly coloured ball across the narrow strip of water that divided them. Lee caught it and threw it back.

It was the signal for all kinds of exchanges. Some were gifts, others swops. They managed to increase their depleted rice supply by exchanging it for some of the medical supplies Lan thought they could spare; grandmother got a chicken for a clock she'd kept hidden away in the black bundle.

Small things were thrown across, more valuable ones swung across in plastic buckets on the end of a line. Toys and silly notes with sweets or chocolates were tossed back and forth and Lee thought it was a little like getting lucky money for Chinese New Year.

During the general air of celebration Lee suddenly felt a damp patch on his jeans where he'd had his leg pressed against the side of the boat. He looked down and saw a pool of water by his feet and realised water was oozing between two of the side planks.

'Grandfather, look!' he said, tugging at the old man's arm to attract his attention in the noise around them.

Grandfather looked where Lee was pointing then raised a finger to his lips. 'Ssh! Don't attract too much attention. That leak could have been there for ages but with so many people on this side of the boat it is lower in the water than usual. Get me some old cloth. Anything will do.'

Lee returned with a shirt he'd always hated. Grandfather had brought a hammer and nails from the engine-house and a piece of wood from an old packing-case.

'Stuff the cloth as tightly as you can into the crack,' he said.

Lee did as he was told and grandfather jammed it further in, using the point of a nail before he nailed the wood on and the trickle of water dried up. He rubbed some water and dust over the board so that it wouldn't attract attention.

'That should do for now,' he said, 'until we can do a proper job. Lee, don't mention this to anyone. Some people might worry about it and there really is no need.'

Lee nodded and forgot all about it when he heard they were to eat the chicken.

During the night, to make navigation safer, the two boats moved apart but the following day the sea was so calm it was decided to lash them together. This had the added advantage that they could run under the power of one engine and save valuable fuel. Ropes were thrown across and secured in the bow and stern of each boat and fenders hung out in the centre where the curved outline of the boats touched.

No sooner were the ropes secured than Quan sprang onto the gunwale and dropped easily onto the deck of the other boat.

'Come on,' he shouted to Lee.

Lee jumped up to follow but his father put a hand on his arm to stop him.

'It's too dangerous and if you go, Tam will want to and she's too small.'

'I'm not,' Tam said firmly, 'I'm six.'

'See what I mean?'

So while the other children charged about making a great nuisance of themselves after days of confinement, Lee had to sit and watch until he could bear it no longer and went off to help Trinh with the engine.

As evening drew near, the ropes were cast off again and the two boats eased apart until they could just make out each other's navigation lights.

A moment later Hue panicked. 'Where's Quan?'

Her husband, Minh, looked about him and then picked his way amongst the other families to see if Quan was with some of the other children but he came back looking anxious.

'I can't see him anywhere and some of the others said he was going to hide on the other boat until we cast off.'

'Silly boy,' Hue said tolerantly, nursing the baby. 'Can you shout across to them to be sure he's all right?'

Minh looked across. It was dark and he could only just make out the lights bobbing along. 'Too far off, they wouldn't hear me above the noise of the engine.'

'I just hope he gets fed, that's all,' Hue said.

'I shouldn't worry about that,' Chi smiled quietly, 'when have you ever known Quan go hungry? My brother can charm birds out of trees when he wants something.'

'Don't worry,' her father said to Hue, putting an arm round her shoulder, 'we'll get him back tomorrow. All the same, it's a silly trick to play and I shall tell him so.'

As Lee wrapped his blanket around him that night, he felt the days had become fuller now they had the company of the other boat even though his father wouldn't let him go on it.

SEVEN

Lee woke violently from his sleep as a sharp movement of the boat threw him hard against its wooden side.

'Is there a storm?' he asked as he rubbed his head.

'Go back to sleep if you can,' his father replied.

'Will it be a typhoon?' Lee persisted.

'We're on the edge of a storm. Grandfather says it will pass us.'

'What if it doesn't?' Kim said as she stirred lazily in her sleep.

'It will,' mother said quietly. Tam lay fast asleep curled up on her lap.

Grandmother sat with her back to the cabin, her cheeks hollow, her eyes wide as she listened to the gathering sound of the wind around them as she had on many nights when grandfather had been out alone in the boat. She had known the wind as her enemy since she was a young girl.

'Where's grandfather?' Lee asked. He was wide awake now.

'With Trinh. They're both in the stern,' father said.

'I think I'll go and see what he's doing,' Lee said as he pulled himself upright on the pitching deck. As soon as he was above the level of the gunwale the wind tugged at his hair.

'Go carefully,' father cautioned but the wind whipped the words away.

The square sail bulged out and its line rattled against the thin wood of the mast as Lee made his way carefully past the engine-house to the stern well. Trinh was leaning heavily on the tiller against the pull of a strong sea. Grandfather sat cross-legged in the well. He was busy hammering at one of the plastic buckets they used for hauling up sea-water.

Lee squatted down beside him. 'Why are you doing that?'

Grandfather's reply came out in spurts between the effort of the blows. 'I want . . . to get the bottom . . . out of some of these . . . in case we need extra sea-anchors.'

'What's a sea-anchor?'

'You tie a line to it, drop it overboard and the drag of the water through it slows you down, so you don't drift too much.'

'Can I help?'

Grandfather passed him a bucket and Lee opened his clasp-knife to cut it.

'Do you think the weather's going to get worse?'

'No,' said grandfather, though he didn't look at Lee as he spoke, 'but there's no harm in being prepared.'

'If the wind gets much stronger,' Trinh said from above them, 'we'll have to run with it. Strong winds never blow the way you want to go, always the opposite way!'

Grandfather just shook his head by way of reply. In all they finished four buckets. 'We've got a canvas anchor, that makes five. Better not use any more buckets or we'll have nothing left for pulling up water.' He pulled himself to his feet. 'Shall I drop the sail?' he asked Trinh.

'Yes,' Trinh agreed, 'and start the engine. I'll bring her round slowly.'

Lee scrambled up on to the cabin-roof after grandfather, who still seemed totally sure-footed, even now the boat was bucking and rearing under him. He expertly gathered the sail with one arm as he lowered it with the other and Lee helped him lash the two cross spars firmly together.

Down in the cabin itself it was difficult to keep from being thrown against the engine but at least it started without too much trouble.

As they came up on deck grandfather waved to Trinh. Trinh nodded grimly back. The tiller was biting into his side and it took all his strength to control it and bring the boat gently round so that the wind blew from the stern. The boat was rolling now in the cross-wind.

'We should have listened to the forecast,' grandfather muttered as they rejoined the family.

'It's Quan's radio,' father pointed out, 'and with him not being here we all forgot.'

'Has anything been seen of the other boat?' Hue asked through the darkness.

'Not for several hours,' grandfather said. 'With this wind it isn't safe to be too close. He'll be all right.'

Shortly after they felt the first spots of rain. After the hot, dry, salty days the cool blobs falling on dry skin produced a wonderful sensation. Lee shut his eyes and tilted his head up towards them so that he could feel each drop land on his face. Then the drops joined together, trickled slowly down and he licked them off greedily with his tongue.

At first they carried salt with them but as the rain grew stronger the taste was purer, the purest water he'd tasted since they left. The shower turned into a deluge. With the wind behind it, it came at them horizontally. People shampooed the water into their hair and on their bodies. They became truly salt-free again. But grandfather, with his more practical mind, was busy thinking of the long term.

'Help me rig the spare sail,' he shouted.

It wasn't easy with a slippery deck and the wind gaining strength every second but the water was too precious to waste. It took six men to hold the sail at all and just as they thought they had it secured, it broke loose from the ropes and flapped angrily at them. After several more attempts they got it rigged by tying one side to the engine-house roof and the other to a beam that ran across the deck. This way, the water collected could run straight into the plastic storage bottles.

'None too soon either,' Hung pointed out, 'we'd very little left.'

The whole family climbed underneath the shelter to get a little protection from the driving rain now that the novelty had worn off. Although their main sail had holes this had more and rivers of rain poured through, especially when the wind got beneath it and tippped it the wrong way.

'The storm's getting worse,' Lee said to grandfather.

'I'm afraid so,' he nodded, 'but I think the worst is still to come.'

'But we decided to set out at this time of year because the typhoon season is over,' father said irritably as if nature had deliberately played a trick on them.

'You can never be certain. But if this had to happen, I wish we'd been nearer one of the islands like Hainan or better still the coast of China. At least then we could have got close in for shelter.'

There was no question of anyone sleeping now. Not only was the motion of the boat too violent, many people were being sick again, but the noise of the wind and rain was too loud. The howling wind which swirled round them sent waves chasing after them over the sides of the boat.

'With so many on board we're riding too low for this kind of weather. The bilge-pump will have a struggle to get the water out again,' grandfather said, and his face suddenly looked much older to Lee.

'The engine doesn't sound too good either,' he put in and they both listened carefully. The waves had grown much larger so that they lifted the stern clear of the water, allowing the propeller to race only to plunge it back beneath the waves and producing a great strain on the engine which wasn't in a condition to take it.

'We have to keep it running. That's the only way we can keep the wind and the waves coming from the stern. If we don't we'll be swamped in a matter of minutes. I'll go and help Trinh with the sea-anchors.' Grandfather rose to his feet.

Lee got up to follow him. 'Can I help too?'

'No,' the old man said, 'there's nothing you can do at the moment and you'll be safer here.'

The sail above them whipped and cracked back and forth in the wind.

'I can't keep this up much longer,' Hung said as he took away the half-filled bottle.

As he spoke two of the lines holding the sail snapped and it flew up into the air like a malignant flag held only by the cabin. But the force with which it moved broke off the mast as easily as if it had been a match. Many hands tried to grab the remains of the mast and the sail to prevent more damage but although they managed to hold the sail, the mast slipped off the cabin-roof and disappeared over the side.

As the storm's intensity continued to increase it was difficult to sit on the wet planks. It seemed as if the boat itself was determined to toss them all out into the foaming, churning sea around them. It bucked and reared so sharply that people lunged painfully into each other and the rain, which had once been so welcome, stung the hands and faces with its ferocity.

All over the boat people were crying out from fear and pain as they rolled helplessly into each other or were dashed against the solid sides of the boat; their possessions adding to the confusion as they fell around in hopeless confusion.

Lee gripped the gunwale as hard as he could and was sick over the side but before he could pull his head back in the sea suddenly threw the boat in the air. His chin crashed down hard on the gunwale and he tasted blood. But his bones were bruised and aching from the buffeting they'd received in the never-ending motion so that he hardly noticed.

By now he was convinced the boat could stand very little more of this and that soon they would all be pitched overboard. Tam was clinging to her mother, both of them were sobbing. Father had one arm round mother and the other round Kim, who had her eyes closed as if what she couldn't see wouldn't harm her. Only grandmother sat still and silent, clutching one of the big, black bundles, the other had rolled away somewhere.

As if to echo Lee's own thoughts a voice cut through the racket of the elements. 'We're breaking up!'

Lee managed with some of the others to scramble across the pitching deck, mostly on his hands and knees. A man was waving a torch about and in its beam Lee could see the constant motion of the boat had eased out the nails from the temporary patch he'd put on with grandfather that afternoon.

The cloth was hanging half out and water was pouring in through the crack which was even wider now so that water not only ran down the side and into the bilges but also across the soaking wet deck in a great stream.

'We're sinking!' the man kept screaming at the top of his voice and some of the others took up his cry; men and women weeping hysterically.

'We've got to get out before it goes down,' the man shouted and clambered awkwardly up on to the engine-house roof. 'If we don't we'll be sucked down with it.' His fingers feverishly plucked at the wet ropes which held the coracle.

But before he could even untie one of the knots the full force of the wind caught him, he slid off the roof and crashed down to the deck. The torch slipped from his grasp and rolled into the scuppers where it lay, half submerged, giving an eerie light that made the people's faces look like skulls before it flickered and died.

As they were once again plunged into darkness others clambered over his body in their haste to get to the coracle.

'Stop that!' a voice roared out.

They froze and looked up to see grandfather standing on the cabin-roof between them and the coracle. His feet apart, one hand held tightly to the remains of the mast while the other brandished a metal spar.

'The first person to touch a rope gets this across his

61

hand,' he shouted.

'Don't listen to him!'

The man who had called out stretched out his hand towards the coracle and grandfather, true to his word, brought the spar crashing down. The man just had time to whip back his hand before the spar splintered a corner of the cabin.

Certain the old man meant what he said, they all drew back but they were still determined to find some way of saving themselves. Their panic so great, these normally intelligent, unselfish, peaceable men sought anything that gave them a chance no matter how slender and, having found it, were prepared to kill anyone who took it away from them again.

One fell over one of the water bottles Hung had re-filled and snatched it up. 'This would keep a man afloat if it was empty,' he shouted. He unscrewed the cap and began tipping the water out.

'It might,' grandfather roared from above them, 'if you could hang on to it out there but you won't be able to!'

But nobody heard him. They fought each other in a desperate attempt to get hold of one of the bottles and then began trying to shake the contents out. Water splashed over their legs and feet.

'You know that won't work!'

Lee turned and saw his father, shaking with anger, his wet hair plastered tight to his skull. Lee had never seen him looking so determined.

'With one of those bottles you'll be swept away in seconds. But even if you managed to hang on and survive the storm what would you do for food and water? If you aren't drowned, you'd die of starvation and thirst.'

All but one of the men carried on with what they were doing.

'And what about your wives and families? When you've jumped overboard with your stupid bottle, what happens to them?'

At that they all stopped and stood for a moment looking guilty and foolish.

'Whatever is going to happen,' father went on, pressing the advantage now he had their attention, 'the only chance we have is together. What we ought to be doing, instead of fighting each other is baling out. Use anything you can lay hands on, tin cans, cooking pots, rice-bowls even, to throw the water back over the side.'

There was a brief pause and then everybody set to work. The empty water bottles rolled across the deck forgotten as people bent their backs to scoop up the water and chuck it overboard. Grandfather climbed down off the roof and Lee was pleased to see him clap father round the shoulder before he too joined in and baled as hard as he could.

Lee was using one of the few buckets not being used as a sea-anchor and as he emptied over the side he thought he saw some lights quite close to them. At first he thought they might be the lights of another cargo ship until he realised they must belong to their companion boat which they hadn't seen since the storm began.

'Grandfather, look out there!'

Grandfather shaded his eyes against the rain but could see nothing at first until a wave lifted her back up into view. 'Look at the list on her!' he gasped.

Lee could see that unlike their boat which managed to recover from each roll, the other boat was tilting over violently to one side, her shoulder dipping beneath the waves.

'She must have shipped an awful lot of water. Their engine must have failed because they've tried to use their sail.' It hung from the broken mast in tatters. 'They're sinking.'

The closer it came, the clearer it was that the boat was drifting hopelessly out of control. Nobody stood at the helm.

'Her rudder must have been broken off by the storm,' grandfather said.

'She's heading straight for us,' father said quietly.

'If she hits us she'll smash us to bits. We'll have to get a rope across to them. That way we might be able to turn her head and get some control over her.'

Everyone had stopped baling to stand gripping the gunwale and watch the floundering boat. Above the noise of the wind and waves they could hear the terrified screams of its passengers and even caught glimpses of their faces.

'Can you see Quan?' Hue shouted but it was impossible to tell one from another.

As grandfather clambered back on to the engine-house roof, he called back to the others, 'Get anything you can to fend her off with.'

They grabbed the empty water bottles, sodden blankets, anything they could find that might dull the impact if the two boats were hurled together and then turned to watch the old man.

Perched precariously on the roof, his first throw fell metres short of the hands that reached out from the second boat.

To Lee it seemed to take hours to pull back the dripping rope and re-coil it. During each moment the gap between the two boats narrowed but at the exact second the rope was thrown again, it went snaking out to a boat that was moved suddenly away from it by a giant wave that crashed over the sides. But no sooner had the rope sunk than the boat began to come at them again; the eye painted on its prow had a malevolent gleam about it.

At the third attempt grandfather managed to get the rope across to the other boat, where eager anxious hands grabbed it and made it fast through the post with a hole in it which all the boats had in the bow.

The boat was still heading straight for them as grandfather wrapped his end of the rope round his forearm. He was a little ahead of the other boat's prow and there was just a slender chance he could pull it off its fatal course, or at least pull it round so that it caught them a glancing rather than a crushing, direct blow.

He heaved on the rope as hard as he could but it made little difference, the boat still plunged towards them.

'Let me help,' Lee said and scrambled up beside the old man. There was only just room for them both. On the roof the movement of the boat felt worse than it had on the deck and it was as much as Lee could do to stay upright let alone pull on the rope. But he grabbed hold of the rope in front of his grandfather.

'Heave!' shouted grandfather. Together they pulled on the coarse rope until Lee's shoulders ached with the effort. For one moment it looked as if they might succeed but then a great wall of water came up between the two boats. Lee watched as the sinking boat disappeared into a trough and he felt the rope burning across his palms as it was dragged away from them by the force of the water.

Lee let go but grandfather, who still had the rope bound tightly around his arm, was caught off balance. He crashed to the roof and slowly but easily the rope tugged him across the shiny, wet cabin-top towards the edge.

Lee tried to stop him by holding on to his clothes but the pull of the sea was too strong for him. Grandfather struggled to free himself of the rope but he had bound it so tightly round himself to pull on it that it was hopelessly entangled digging into the thin flesh of his wiry arms. Every second he was dragged closer to the edge below which was the fuming sea.

Then Lee remembered the clasp-knife. He dug it out of his pocket: the blade glinted as he opened it.

Grandfather's feet had already reached the edge but he managed to brace one of them against the coracle. The rope was turning him as easily as a leaf. If the sea could not get him feet first it was determined to take him head first.

Lee stabbed at the rope but it moved on before he could cut until he saw that it was being pulled over the extreme edge of the cabin-roof. He chopped his knife down on it at that point and sawed for all he was worth. Only a few strands frayed off before the rope moved on again. He tilted the blade at an angle against the movement of the rope, trying to use the strength of the sea to make up for his lack.

The blade began to bite and it was indeed the weight of the sea which snapped the final strands. As it fell into the sea, grandfather, who was now trussed by the free end of the rope like a chicken, fell back exhausted on to the roof. Lee sank to his knees beside him, sobbing with relief as he slowly unwound the rope.

The whole affair had taken barely a minute but as they rose to their knees it was to see the stricken boat being lifted up like a great white whale. For a second it seemed that the sea was considering hurling the two boats together in a final gigantic crash but then it seemed to lose interest. It dropped the sinking boat into another trough and threw a huge wave over it. When it seemed that even then it might recover, a second larger wave caught the boat broadside on and it was rolled over. People and possessions were flung into the water like scraps of paper.

The boat never righted itself again but began to break up in the crashing waves. It seemed impossible that anyone could survive but moments later heads bobbed up amongst the flotsam of planks, food and bedding which littered the surface.

'Get ropes out to them,' yelled Trinh.

Ropes were grabbed and hurled out. The struggling survivors, most of whom could not swim, thrashed about vainly in the black spume. Some ropes were swept back in only to be cast again and again. Others trailed out like streamers.

Those who struggled in the water couldn't see them. Several made instead for the remains of their boat, but then found it impossible to get hold of the slippery, barnacle-covered upturned hull and slipped back into the foaming water. Some came up to try again, spewing

66

out the water they'd been forced to swallow, most did not.

One man, who did see a rope, grabbed it and was being hauled in when a wave lifted him from behind and smashed him viciously against the side of the boat.

Lee watched in horror as the man dropped back into the water his face smashed into an ugly, bloody pulp.

Five were rescued, all of them men. Forty-one men, women and children disappeared without trace. Quan was not amongst the survivors.

EIGHT

Lee woke well before sunrise. The storm had blown itself out during the night. He sat hunched and shivering in his damp blanket. Even with the engine running after the fury of the typhoon there seemed to be an unnatural quiet.

At the height of the storm, seeing another dawn seemed such an unlikely possibility that it was surprising when the sun rose. This was partly because it rose on the wrong side but also because its intensity turned the waves black by contrast.

He rubbed his palms gingerly and felt the blisters raised by the rope. He looked across at grandfather who was still asleep. His face looked longer and thinner than ever. There were dull purple weals on his arms where the rope had gripped him.

There were ugly bruises on Kim's forehead and Tam twitched and murmured in her sleep. Lee's parents slept very close to each other and grandmother had her chin sunk deep in her chest but nobody ever knew when she slept or when she rested.

Lee and the man who had replaced the exhausted Trinh at the tiller were the only two people awake. Even Quan's parents had eventually fallen asleep a couple of hours earlier, mainly from complete nervous exhaustion. The baby, Phan, was somewhere wrapped in amongst them. Only their daughter Chi slept a little apart from the rest of the family as if she was not included in their grief.

The horrors of the night were still very clear in Lee's mind but the one which haunted him most was the unseen death of Quan which had only occurred as the result of a stupid prank.

Lee found it impossible to believe that he would never

see Quan's face ever again. It was still so clear in his mind's eye. He kept looking across expecting to see Quan sleeping in his usual place next to his father and, even knowing he was dead, was surprised to see he was not there.

Although nobody he'd known had died, Lee, like most people of his age and above in Vietnam, was no stranger to death itself. He particularly remembered going shopping with his mother in Cholon one day when they heard a loud explosion. On the way home they passed a block of flats the front of which had been ripped out by the force of the blast. It was an obscene sight. Things never intended for public view were exposed. A mattress pad, its stuffing fluffed out, hung half out of one flat, from another a fully laden table hung suspended in mid-air on three legs. Flames licked round the door of a higher flat from which a man in blood-spattered pyjamas screamed for rescue as he clutched the lifeless body of a child.

The smell of dust and burning hung heavy in the air. People muttered the word, 'Terrorists!' Some helped to search amongst the rubble for survivors but most stood, several still astride their bikes or mopeds, one old man rested his chin on the handlebars of his tri-shaw, like frozen images brought to a halt by the closeness of death and the thankfulness it wasn't theirs.

Above the shouting of the rescuers and the screams of the victims Lee clearly heard the bright whistle of a little bird. High above his head he saw the bird still in its circular bamboo cage which hung from the jagged outline of what had once been a window-frame.

Lee had often remembered the sound of the bird to erase the horrors of that day but now could find nothing to ease his mind. He knew that in spite of Quan's bravado he had lost face when he fell asleep on watch and Lee had never let him off the hook by admitting that he'd done the same thing. Now Lee wanted Quan back and alive so that he could tell him but it was too late and

Lee knew that he would never be able to tell anyone else what he hadn't told Quan before his death. That was a burden Lee must carry.

People began to wake slowly and quietly. There was a sense of uneasiness on the boat. The smell of joss-sticks mingled with that of breakfast as many cupped the sticks between their palms and bowed for deliverance.

The men who had fought over the water bottles sat very still and avoided everybody's eyes by staring at their feet. The five survivors from the sunken boat huddled in a group trying to equate their relief at rescue with their grief for wives, children and brothers lost in the shipwreck, and ending up with a sadness fuelled by their own guilt at having survived at all.

Nobody liked to ask Minh if they could use Quan's radio to listen to the news and weather forecast. Fortunately he switched it on without being asked but although they listened carefully to the weather prospects, the news seemed so remote from their own recent and very real experiences that everybody's minds drifted off into their private thoughts and nobody noticed when the set was switched off.

Very slowly as the morning wore on people began to pick up the pieces of their lives. Long lines were strung out on which to dry clothes and bedding. Belongings which had rolled around in the storm were sorted out and most handed back to their original owners though oddly there remained several things nobody recognised.

For the five new passengers not only had room to be made but as they had no belongings at all the simplest things like razors and rice-bowls also had to be found. All of these were happily handed over as presents and there was no quarrel at all about them sharing in what food had not been ruined by the storm. As Hung collected up the empty water bottles from around the deck, nobody said a word about the hysterical folly and waste of the previous night but the water ration was severely cut that day.

Apart from the patch of deck beneath the still-seeping planks, which Trinh set about patching again, the deck slowly dried out in the heat of the sun and the wooden sides cracked loudly as the moisture was sucked out of them.

Grandfather used the sun to get the boat back on to the correct course. Lee sat beside him in the stern grateful to feel the boat responding easily as it rode the sea again instead of being its victim.

'We've easily lost a day's headway, maybe more,' grandfather grumbled as if they'd suffered some minor inconvenience as he turned the boat.

'Will we go back past the wreck?' Lee asked hoping that they wouldn't because he had a horror of seeing Quan's body floating in the water.

'There's no way of knowing. Sometimes a storm scatters the wreckage so much anyway that you pass it for days, other times it all stays together. We might.'

Just before midday the lookout man on the prow shouted out to them that there was a good deal of stuff floating in the water immediately ahead of them. Grandfather slowed the engine down as they approached the widespread area of flotsam and stopped it altogether as they began to pass amongst it.

Most people, especially Quan's parents, didn't want to look. The five survivors looked in the vain hope they might find a member of their family still alive clinging to a plank but there were no bodies alive or dead just the pathetic reminders of their existence. Blankets, boxes and orange peel bobbed about in the water in a colourful confusion.

Of those who did look many were reduced to tears especially one of the survivors who recognised the blanket his wife had worn round her shoulders when the boat broke up.

Grandfather, used to the sea's cruel ways, had his mind on more practical matters. 'There's water in that bottle!' he shouted and grabbed a boat-hook. It went neatly through the handle and grandfather hauled it aboard triumphantly although some people viewed his action with distaste.

'It's like fumbling in the pockets of a body not yet cold,' one man muttered.

Grandfather, who heard the remark was undismayed. 'We are desperately short of water, is that right, Hung?'

'It is,' Hung confirmed.

'The people this belonged to would far rather we collect the things they no longer need than die ourselves. There's another bottle and there's cooking oil over there!'

After that most people gave a hand and pulled up all manner of things which might prove useful including baulks of timber and blankets.

Lee had joined in reluctantly and was glad when grandfather announced that they had collected everything worth having.

'Start the engine,' he said to Lee.

It started with the usual difficulty and when Lee climbed back up he saw Quan's sister, Chi, lighting a stick of incense she'd set in a plastic bowl with some candlewax. As they moved slowly away she leant over the side and gently dropped the pot into the water. Convinced it would sink, Lee held his breath but when he looked over the stern he saw the pink plastic pot bobbing in their wake as a solitary tribute, the smoke from the stick drifting away in the wind to mix with the fumes of their engine.

When Lee turned back he found that Chi was not looking at the pot but at him. He was suddenly aware of how like her brother she was. The eyes which looked out from beneath the broad forehead could easily have been his eyes and yet there was no impudent jut of her jaw but something much quieter, softer.

He wanted to speak but could think of no words to say to her. He tried to smile his thoughts to her but that wouldn't work either, his face stuck out of embarrassment. He remembered her slightly husky voice from the morning she had started the singing and wanted to make her speak to him now but could find no way of doing it and in a moment she had gone back to rejoin her family.

In the afternoon grandfather climbed up onto the roof to do some fishing. 'Though I doubt there'll be much about after the storm,' he said to Lee as they clambered up.

Perched up there in the sunshine together their roof-top struggle seemed like a nightmare until Lee looked down and saw the splintered wood where the old man had brought the spar down and the chipped paint where his knife had eventually cut through the rope.

Lee lay back on the roof, gazing up at the pure blue of the sky. A single bird wheeled back and forth high above them.

'Grandfather,' he said, pointing up into the sky, 'there's a bird up there, doesn't that mean we're close to land?'

'Not necessarily,' the old man said. 'People like to believe it does always mean that but it isn't true.'

Lee wanted it to be true. He lay there wondering where the bird had come from and, if indeed they were far from land, how it had survived the storm? While he was still thinking these thoughts sleep overtook him and he drifted off.

'Have you ever drunk a fish?'

The voice was his grandfather's. Lee knew that, although he still had his eyes closed and the question was so odd that he thought at first he must be dreaming. But when he opened them it was his real grandfather who sat with his legs over the cabin side holding a fairly large fish.

'The only one I've caught all afternoon,' he said. 'Do you know how to drink one?'

Lee looked baffled. 'You mean put it in a liquidiser?'

'No need. I'll show you. One day this might come in

useful. Lend me that good knife of yours. The one I have every reason to be pleased I gave to you.'

Lee beamed with pride as he handed it over. That was the only reference the old man had made to Lee saving his life.

Grandfather cut along the back of the fish just below its dorsal fin and deep enough to penetrate the muscle. When he tilted the fish towards the incision it filled with a clear liquid. He held it up to Lee's lips. 'Drink it.'

Lee did. It had an odd taste, a little fishy, but was surprisingly pure and salt-free and therefore quite palatable. Only the scales scratching against his lips produced an unpleasant sensation.

Then grandfather did another cut on the other side, millimetres from the fin's root and more liquor appeared.

'You can do the same every few millimetres. You see a fish is mostly water. You can drink it like you just have, straight from the fish, or if you catch several fish, do all the cuts at once and hang them up over a bowl then let the water run out. If you're really in a hurry, do the cuts, wrap the fish in a cloth then twist the cloth and squeeze the water out.'

'Will somebody steer while I have a look at the engine?' Trinh called from the stern.

Now they had no mast on which to raise a sail, they were wholly dependent on the engine so Trinh had begun to nurse it like a baby. He checked far more regularly than was necessary that it had enough fuel, oil and water.

'If it had a nose, he'd wipe it!' grandfather declared. 'You go and steer, Lee.'

Lee was delighted. He'd never been allowed to steer on his own before without anybody sitting beside him. Just at the moment he felt happier if he was doing something because sitting with the family he found it hard to keep his thoughts away from Quan's death especially with Hue crying most of the day.

He'd been steering for only a few moments when he saw Chi making her way round the engine-house towards him. Lee could feel again the awkwardness he'd experienced the last time she was near him. After all Kim and Tam were the only girls he'd ever had anything to do with and sisters didn't really count.

As she got close he noticed for the first time she wore the traditional black trousers which these days were mostly worn only by the older women. His sisters, Kim and Tam, both wore jeans, much to grandmother's disapproval. Maybe the old-fashioned style of dress meant that Chi's parents had brought her up very strictly. Lee knew that in some families girls were not allowed to speak to a boy unless their marriage had been arranged.

Lee deliberately focused his eyes on the horizon. He didn't speak and nor did she. She sat on the gunwale a short distance from him. She just seemed to want to be with him but he couldn't think why and her silence made him as uncomfortable as her presence.

In the end Lee could bear it no longer. 'I'm very sorry about Quan,' he said quietly, still not taking his eyes off the horizon.

Chi didn't reply. Instead she bowed her head slightly in acknowledgement. Lee didn't dare turn his head, but tried to see out of the corner of his eye, if he'd upset her but although he couldn't see her eyes her expression seemed unchanged.

Without looking up she said, 'The baby, Phan, is ill now.' Lee was quite startled by the unexpected deepness and strength of her voice. 'Now my mother is losing her milk. Last night didn't help. The nurse, Lan, has brought dried milk with her but the baby won't take it and he's getting very weak.'

Lee had grown so used to Phan's crying that it was only now that Chi had mentioned it he realised they had become more whimpers than cries.

'What does Lan say?' Lee asked wondering why Chi was telling him all this.

75

'She says there's nothing to be done. Mother must keep on trying and hope for the best.' She looked over the stern of the boat. 'You aren't steering very straight.'

Lee glanced back. It was true he left almost a zigzag across the water. He tried to concentrate more but he couldn't help thinking about Chi's matter-of-fact tone.

There was a long silence before Chi spoke again. 'My parents have lost Quan, their first-born son, now it seems they may lose their second son too. I suppose it's understandable they don't have much time to spend on their daughter.'

NINE

'How much longer before we reach land?' Lee asked.

Grandfather shook his head. 'We would have reached land now but for the typhoon.'

'But that was two days ago.'

'But after the typhoon with no charts we have little idea of where we are, but if we keep going in this direction we should reach the China coast sooner or later. Mind you if I'm wrong, it's next stop Japan or even America!'

'Could we really sail all the way to America?' Lee asked wide-eyed at the prospect.

'I doubt it,' grandfather smiled, 'though some boats made it to Australia without touching land once.'

There was no doubt they were in drastic need of water and a change of diet. Complete lack of fruit and vegetables combined with constant exposure to the salt-laden sea air had caused skin irritations to change into weeping abscesses. Diarrhoea was rife.

'But in these conditions,' Lan continually pointed out to the people she tried to help, 'what else can you expect?'

Everyone was getting weak and low. Many cried all day and all night. Only Phan's cries grew weaker and weaker. Tempers were growing very frayed.

'If a girl like you is to become a good wife and mother you must learn to help with the work,' grandmother said sharply to Kim.

'Even if we survive, Dong is still in Cholon,' Kim said tearfully.

'Dong? Who is this Dong?'

'You know very well,' mother interposed in an attempt to try and keep the peace. 'Dong was the boy Kim was very friendly with back home.'

Grandmother sniffed. 'Young girls waited until they were old enough for marriage before being friendly with boys in my day.'

'But not in mine,' mother said gently. 'Things are changing.'

'But not for the best it seems when a young girl is too proud to help with the cooking and washing,' grandmother snapped back.

Mother bit back her reply. 'Isn't it time you collected your water ration?' she said to Kim.

Kim made her way to the stern, glad to be away from the constant criticism she got from her grandmother, if only for a few moments. She watched Hung carefully measuring out water for each of the short line of people she'd joined.

Accidentally one man, at the head of the queue, stood on Hung's hand. Hung lashed out at the man, one of the North Vietnamese they'd rescued, and shouted at him. 'Peasant!'

The man swung at Hung and a full-scale fight broke out in which one of the few remaining water bottles was knocked over, spilling the precious contents over the deck.

Trinh it was who pulled them apart. 'What's going on?' he demanded.

'That fool says the war was all our fault,' Hung said breathing heavily.

'So it was,' the North Vietnamese man insisted, 'if you had not been traitors to your country and let in the Americans. . .'

'Stop all this nonsense!' Trinh snapped. 'We're all in the same boat now and it happens to be my boat. But if there's any more trouble I'll tip you both over the side!'

'I won't cause trouble if he doesn't call me a peasant!' the man said and stalked off, leaving Hung looking surly.

Wherever Lee went Chi went also. She had become his permanent but silent shadow. Lee was still feeling upset and guilty about Quan's death and Chi's constant

78

presence only served as an uncomfortable reminder which he would rather have done without.

Tam was quick to notice. 'Your girl-friend's waiting for you,' she said when she noticed Chi hanging about on the engine-house roof just above them.

Lee rather crossly told her to shut up but that only earned him a rebuke from his father and a further bombardment with silly remarks from Tam. As he was due to go on watch on the cabin in a few minutes anyway, he decided to go just to stop Tam being silly.

Chi appeared not to notice his arrival at all. She just sat looking out to sea but there was no doubt in Lee's mind that on such a small boat she couldn't have failed to hear Tam's remarks which made him all the more uncomfortable. If only she'd talk it would make things easier, he thought, but didn't really believe it.

When Chi tapped him on the shoulder he almost jumped out of his skin. She was pointing to the distant horizon on her side of the boat. Lee could just make out the pale, bellying, 'bent triangle' sails of a junk set to sail across their course. He called out to Trinh who was at the helm. Grandfather climbed up beside him for a better view and Lee noticed Chi slipped away as soon as she realised he was coming.

'Perhaps it means we're getting close to land,' Lan shouted out, but her husband, Khai, didn't look nearly so convinced.

Everyone stood up to admire the boat, only the third they had seen since they set out. Some waved and cheered but Lee noticed grandfather keeping a very keen eye on the junk.

'What's the matter, grandfather?'

'Nothing, so long as she keeps to her course.'

'If they come close they might be able to help with food and water.'

'They might,' the old man said quietly, 'but I doubt it.'

Lee looked back towards the junk. There was no

doubt about it, her head was coming round. They'd spotted the fishing-boat and were coming straight for it. Grandfather got up and began to move towards the engine-room.

'What are you going to do?' Lee asked.

'Better to be on the safe side,' he said and disappeared only to reappear with a couple of hammers. One he gave to Lee's father. 'Help me loosen these planks,' he said kneeling on the deck just forward of the engine-house, clawing at the nails.

'Why, what's going to happen?' father asked as he bent to help.

'I can't be sure,' grandfather said as the first nails squealed out of the wood, 'that may be a perfectly innocent junk but I don't like the way it altered course when it spotted us. Most people would rather have nothing to do with the likes of us except one kind of people, what some would call pirates.'

'Pirates?' Lee echoed unable to keep the astonishment out of his voice.

'They're really ordinary merchantmen who can't resist robbing helpless people like us for a little bit of easy money. That makes them pirates.' He stood back from his work and addressed the crowd which had gathered to watch him. 'Everything of value and all the young girls must go down there now!'

As they looked down into the hole he opened up, down into slopping, stinking bilge-water in the belly of the boat they couldn't believe he was serious and there were murmurs of protest and laughter.

'If they're honest men, nothing will happen,' grandfather insisted, 'and I won't mind being called a fool, but if I'm right they'll take everything of value from this boat and probably one or two young girls for good measure!'

'He's quite right,' Trinh joined to emphasise the point. 'They can be brutal.'

After that nobody argued. A cardboard box was found

and as it was passed round each person dropped in watches, jewellery, small pieces of gold even, then the whole thing was stuffed unceremoniously down the hole.

'Now girls. Quick there's no time to waste. If they get much closer they'll be able to see what we're doing.'

One by one the girls, many sobbing with fear, climbed carefully down through the deck into an area so small they were forced to lie half in the stinking water.

Only Chi held back. 'I can't go down there,' she said her normally strong voice shaking with terror.

Lee was very surprised. He couldn't ever remember Chi registering any emotion. She braced herself at the very edge of the hole and her whole body seemed to shake with fear as she looked first at her parents and then at Lee for support. Minh seemed unsure of himself, his eyes avoided hers. Hue, on the other hand, didn't seem to have noticed anything unusual was happening and was still intent on nursing Phan. Lee wished there was something he could do or say but couldn't think of anything and in any case couldn't see why Chi didn't realise she would be far safer below deck than above it if these men really turned out to be pirates.

In the end it was Kim who came to the rescue. 'Chi, you must come down or they can't nail up the hole, then we'll all be caught. Come on down, it's not so bad once you're in here, I promise.'

Kim held out her hand to Chi who took it warily with one hand, the other was stuffed in her mouth to prevent her crying out aloud and Lee could see tears rolling down her cheeks. Then she took a deep breath and climbed in with the rest.

Hurriedly grandfather slid the boards back into position and began to nail them down again.

'Don't nail them right down,' Chi pleaded from below.

'It has to look right to them if they board us,' grandfather said and drove the last nail firmly home. He rubbed over the nail-heads with his hand to try and disguise the fact that they'd ever been disturbed then he put his head close to the boards. 'Keep very still and don't forget the slightest sound can be heard up here too. You may be able to hear what's going on but we'll tell you when it's safe to come up again.'

'There's very little air down here, grandfather,' Kim's voice was muffled by the timber but still quite clear which proved grandfather's point.

'I know,' he replied, 'but it might be a little better if we have to stop, though if we have to shut down the engine the bilge-pump will stop also and you may feel the level of water rise very slightly. But don't be alarmed, it won't be much.'

The old man stood up and waved everybody away. 'Back to your places and try to behave as normally as possible.'

Trinh, grandfather and Lee all made for the stern and the man who'd been steering made his way back to his family.

'I suppose there's no chance that we could outrun them?' grandfather said to Trinh.

'Not with our poor little engine,' Trinh replied, shaking his head. 'They have enough sail alone to catch us and probably a powerful diesel engine that works, besides.'

'It would probably only convince them that we were worth catching if we started to run for it anyway,' the old man said. 'We'll just have to take our chances.'

TEN

If the men on the junk were honest they must have thought they were getting a poor reception for when three of them waved nobody on the fishing-boat moved, let alone raised a hand in greeting.

As it drew close, the distinctive sails billowed down and it cruised in using its engine. Lee thought it odd that a boat that appeared so welcome on the horizon got more menacing the closer it got with its after-deck towering above them.

A fat man stood up there watching everything and as they came alongside he hailed Trinh and called out in a voice that was reedy for such bulk, 'Can we come aboard?'

Trinh's only response was a shrug meant to indicate they could please themselves and probably would.

'Cut your engine,' the fat man shouted in a tone that made it difficult to decide whether it was a suggestion or an order.

Trinh did as he was told and there was silence except for the idling engine on the junk which drifted closer and closer. Men stood waiting with rope fenders. Lee wished he was young enough to hold his grandfather's hand but stood a little closer to him as the next best thing.

In spite of the fenders the junk hit them with a bump which threw the people on the fishing-boat off-balance. On the second of impact boat-hooks swung across and bit into the gunwale of Trinh's boat.

The fat man was first aboard. He brought with him a tall, thin man with a vacant, staring expression and another whose face seemed stuck in an idiotic grin that Lee didn't like the look of at all.

'Are you the Boss man?' the fat man said to Trinh as

he made his way into the stern well.

Trinh nodded.

'Are you from Vietnam?'

Trinh nodded again.

'Heading for Hong Kong?' The fat man smiled, he knew all the answers, Trinh didn't even bother to nod. 'You don't seem very talkative. Is there anything you need, are you short of water?' he asked pointing down at the plastic containers lying empty on the deck.

'Yes, we are,' Trinh said quietly.

'Oh? We have plenty. Perhaps we could do a deal? What would you say a litre of fresh water was worth to you? Mmm?'

Lee thought he saw Trinh tremble a little as he replied, 'I don't know.'

'I'm sure we can come to some arrangement,' the fat man said with a smile that looked more like a leer. He turned to the men he'd left on the junk. 'Fill these bottles,' he ordered, then he pointed straight at Lee. 'You boy, take them across.'

Lee froze, too terrified to move.

'Didn't you hear me, boy?' the leer stayed in place, 'Take the bottles and get them filled!'

Lee still didn't move but tried to edge slightly behind his grandfather.

'I'll go,' the old man said pleasantly and stooped to pick up the bottles.

'No, you won't. The boy will go, won't you boy?'

Grandfather, seeing there was no other way urged Lee forward with his hand. 'Go on, Lee, you'll be all right.'

'Of course you will,' the fat man's leer widened even further and the sun glistened off the top of his bald head.

Lee fumbled for the bottles. He managed to pick them up but his hands were shaking so much one fell, rattled across the deck ending up at the fat man's feet.

'Take them all,' he said sweetly as he kicked it back at Lee.

When Lee had all the bottles he staggered clumsily along the boat. The man with the vacant expression took the bottles and tossed them carelessly towards the junk. All landed on its deck except one which dropped short, fell between the two boats and was ground to powder by their weight as they rose and fell together on the slack sea.

Lee was still watching when he felt the man grab him and throw him towards the junk equally casually. In the split second he was in the air Lee couldn't help thinking about the fate of that bottle. But he needn't have worried. He landed with a thump on the deck and whilst he was still rubbing his bruised shoulder, rough hands grabbed him and dragged him to his feet. A short man with few teeth held him tightly by both arms.

'Now,' shouted the fat man, 'while they fill the bottles we'll discuss the price. Gold is what I'm asking. All the gold on this boat. I know refugees like to plead poverty but I wouldn't advise any tricks if you want the boy and the water back on this boat.'

As Lee started to fill the water bottles from a tap on the front of a huge water barrel he couldn't help wondering if it was really worth his while bothering. Knowing that everything of value was stored away below deck and that it couldn't be revealed without disclosing the hiding place of the girls, Lee couldn't see how he, or the water, would ever get back on board.

The two men were busy searching the bundles of possessions that lay on the deck. There weren't many and it didn't take long to examine them all.

'Found anything?' the fat man asked as they returned. They both shook their heads. 'Nothing at all?' He wagged a fat forefinger at the passengers. 'I think you'd all better try a little harder. Don't forget the boy is still on my boat with the water you so desperately need! Rings, watches, anything will do,' he said reasonably, 'as long as it's gold and there's enough of it.'

The two men strolled back amongst the frightened

people. Lee was trembling so much he slopped the water over the deck of the junk.

'I should be careful what you're doing,' hissed his toothless guard, 'you may be staying and then you'll have the mess to clear up!'

This possibility was so real in Lee's mind that although he'd only filled two bottles he stopped pouring and began to wonder if there was any chance of escaping by jumping back to his own boat. He dismissed this as pointless, the three men still aboard it would probably just throw him back again. They might not be so accurate with their aim a second time. He just had to hope they would find something to satisfy their greed.

'That woman is wearing a ring!' the fat man called out.

The man with the idiot grin looked to see where he was pointing then extended his bony hand towards grandmother who stood looking defiantly at him.

'You can't take it,' she said quietly, 'and anyway it isn't gold!'

I'll be the judge of that,' the fat man said, 'and as for taking it, it's only a question of whether he takes it with or without your finger. He won't mind, he's a simple lad.'

The man's grin spread a little as he produced a long, evil-looking knife which must have come straight from the kitchen. It glinted in the sunlight as he took a step towards her. Quietly grandmother took off the ring and dropped it on the deck. It fell with a clatter and for a moment the man looked as if he would bury the knife in her thin old body but at the last moment he bent down and picked up the ring instead.

'Now, that's a start,' the fat man said pleasantly, 'but it's only bought you one bottle of water and it certainly won't get you the boy back. That man, the one in the bow!'

Lan's husband, Khai, blinked as he realised who he meant.

86

'Why are you wearing shoes? Nobody else is. Take a look!'

Khai pressed himself against the gunwale as if to escape but the two men pushed their way roughly through the people and the one with the vacant expression grabbed Khai's ankles and heaved. Khai fell to the deck with a thud. The man tore off the shoes and looked inside but found nothing.

'The heels, you fool, try the heels,' the fat man shouted fiercely, the smile had gone as if a shutter had dropped.

Khai scrambled to his feet and tried to grab the shoes back. The grinning man picked him up bodily and dropped him over the side of the boat as easily as if he'd been emptying a pail of slops.

There was a splash and a cry as Khai hit the water. Lan ran to the side screaming. It had all happened so quickly that nobody could really believe it. Hung was the first to act, he grabbed a rope and was about to throw it to Khai who was thrashing about in the water as the two boats slowly drifted away from him when the fat man shouted, 'Drop it!'

Hung looked up and realised the man held a cumbersome-looking gun in his flabby paw and although it looked like a relic of the Second World War he knew the fat man would use it. The rope dropped to the deck. Lan howled in misery.

'Let's see what your husband's been hiding,' the fat man said. With a triumphant shout he clambered past the engine-house and snatched up the shoe. He twisted the heel which revealed a hidden compartment then he tipped the shoe up and gold coins fell into the fat man's hand. There was even more in the second heel. 'Ten *taels* of gold. Your husband was a foolish man not to hand that over straight away.'

'Now you've got the money can we throw the rope? Khai can't swim.'

The fat man looked over the side at the receding figure

of Khai whose thrashing was already growing more feeble. 'I doubt he'll need to much longer. However, I'm quite prepared to put him out of his misery, though at this distance I couldn't be certain one shot would do it.'

The rest of the women hid their faces in horror at the prospect as Lan slumped to the deck sobbing.

'Oh, well, just as you wish,' the fat man shrugged, 'but now your husband's gone there's no point in you staying on this leaky old tub. You'd better come with us.'

'No!' Lan screamed as he put his hand under her arm and dragged her to her feet. The tall thin man picked Lan up and walked across the deck with her still kicking and screaming. Several passengers on the fishing-boat made a move towards him but the fat man waved his gun.

'I wouldn't do anything foolish,' he said and they parted to let the man through. He threw Lan across to the junk where she landed close to Lee. He stooped to help her up but the toothless man hissed at him, 'Don't worry, we'll take good care of her!'

Two of the crew dragged her, still screaming, below the deck. Then Lee jumped as the fat man shouted across to him, 'You haven't filled many bottles yet. You'd better get a move on.' Then he eased himself with difficulty down into the engine-room.

Lee thought everyone had forgotten about him and like Lan he was destined to stay on the junk. He quickly began to fill up as many bottles as he could.

The fat man reappeared from the engine-room holding their last remaining cans of kerosene which he calmly dropped over the side. Unlike the water bottles they'd salvaged from the wreck these had so little air trapped in them that they sank immediately in a flurry of bubbles as Trinh and grandfather watched, grim-faced, from the stern.

'Just in case you think of trying to follow us,' the fat

man explained then he turned back to Lee, 'jump if you're going to.'

Lee bent down to collect the four bottles he'd managed to fill.

'Leave those there,' the man shouted. 'You'll have enough trouble getting across yourself.'

Lee walked to the edge of the deck. He looked down and saw the junk relentlessly crushing the fenders of the smaller boat. If he missed his footing that would be where he would end up. He felt a glaze of cold sweat on the back of his neck.

'Get off my boat,' the fat man ordered. He'd climbed up on to the engine-house roof with the other man who was clutching Quan's radio, the only other item of value he'd been able to find. 'I'm going to count to three and if you aren't off my boat I'll shoot you down. One!'

Lee remained rooted to the spot. Although Lee knew the man meant what he said and his brain was telling him he had to jump or die anyway, his body was rendered immobile by the distance between the two boats and the distorted fenders squashed between them.

'Two!'

'Lee, jump, you can make it!'

He looked when he heard his father's voice. His face was imploring Lee to try. Without taking his eyes off his father Lee flung himself off the edge of the junk. But the jump was too short. His knees hit the fishing-boat's gunwale. For a second his body seemed to hang suspended in mid-air as if any moment he might slither down the smooth planks to be crushed by the boats. At the last moment he threw his weight forwards and somersaulted painfully onto the deck.

'Good boy, Lee,' his father said as he helped him up. Lee was crying like a baby from fright and pain. 'It's all right now, Lee.' His father squatted beside him brushing Lee's tears away into his hair. 'You're safe.'

Through his own tears Lee saw those of his father. They hugged each other tightly. They had not been so close since Lee was a baby.

While Lee was recovering, the two men had leapt across back to the junk and the fat man was standing beside the water bottles.

'Ten *taels* only buys two bottles,' he said and tossed them across to the fishing-boat. They fell heavily on the deck and one split so that it left a dark trail of water as it rolled. He nudged the other two overboard with his toe and tossed the empty ones after them.

Lee covered his ears with his hands so that he couldn't hear the grinding noise they made as they splintered into fragments. When he uncovered them he heard the junk's diesel start up and saw her slide slowly away. Above the noise of the engine, from somewhere in the bowels of the junk, Lee could hear Lan's agonised screams then the grey sails were unfurled and the junk made off.

Trinh had already started the engine and was heading back for the spot where they'd last seen Khai but although they cruised around the area for some time there was no sign of him now.

Grandfather heaved the nails out of the deck planks as soon as he thought the junk was a safe distance away. The girls slowly crawled out, a pitiful sight. Their hands, faces, hair and clothes were dripping with foul-smelling slime from the bilge-water and oil in the bottom of the boat. Some had also been sick in the rank atmosphere. Most were crying and some, now the ordeal was over, were hysterical.

Grandmother despite the differences she had had with Kim in the past, or perhaps because of them, hugged her hard and wept over her. Mother was hugging Tam, trying to wipe the mixture of tears and oil from her face.

Only Chi stood totally alone. She stood at the rail, her back to everyone including her parents, her eyes dry, her face calm as she stared out to sea after the departing junk.

ELEVEN

Next day grandfather called another meeting. Apart from Minh and Hue Duong, who took no interest in anything but the baby, everybody else squatted on the deck looking up to grandfather and Trinh.

'The water shortage is so bad we are going to have to further reduce the daily ration,' grandfather announced. Lee looked at the deck. Grandfather, noticing his discomfort, quickly added, 'You have nothing to reproach yourself with, Lee. No matter how many bottles you'd filled he wouldn't have let you bring them back because without actually killing us, he would rather we died, for obvious reasons. But it does mean the ration must be cut to half a bowl between two people a day.'

There were murmurs of protest but grandfather waved them aside and everybody realised that it was the only sensible thing to do.

'And if that isn't bad enough,' grandfather said, 'Trinh has some worse news for you.'

'We are very short of kerosene after yesterday, all we have left is what was already in the engine and the same applies to engine oil because one of the cans he threw overboard contained all we had. The engine is due for a top-up anyway, it is old and uses more than it should, and if we run it when it's short it'll seize up altogether.'

'Which means that we should only use it in a flat calm,' grandfather said firmly. 'All the more reason for being very cautious about the water. It also means that Trinh and I are going to try and make a makeshift mast out of some of the timber we salvaged. I think that's all unless anybody has any questions or suggestions?'

Hung stood up. 'As we shan't be seeing anything more of Khai and Lan, shouldn't somebody else look after the medical supplies?'

'I could do that,' Lee's mother volunteered.

'Very well,' grandfather nodded, graciously giving permission to a woman of his family to take on the responsibility. 'I think the survivors of the wreck should look through the rest of their possessions to see if there are things they can use, blankets at least.'

Trinh and grandfather set to work straight away and Lee took their turns at the tiller. Although he was very happy to steer, partly because the carpentry being done on the main deck made conditions even more cramped, he was surprised to discover how quickly his arms tired. Despite changing hands as often as he could, his muscles were no longer up to any long physical demands. The lack of exercise and variety of diet were taking their toll on everyone. In the end he was pleased to see Chi coming towards him, anything to take his mind off his aching arms. For once Lee was happy to break the silence that always existed between them.

'Was it horrible, shut in below the deck?' he asked.

Chi looked calmly at the never-ending ocean around them. 'I didn't believe your grandfather when he told us what might happen but what happened on the deck was far worse than being below. It's just that I hate being in confined spaces. I always have since I was small. Once, while my parents were out I accidentally shut myself up in a cupboard.' As she remembered her voice went very low and Lee saw the fear cloud her eyes.

'I'd been playing and I decided to climb into this cupboard, I don't remember why, and then I heard the catch snap down behind me. I banged on the door but of course there was nobody in the flat to hear me. I quickly gave up banging and just sat. Then I started to get hungry and thirsty. Probably if I'd been outside it wouldn't have happened but because I couldn't get anything it grew worse and worse, like being on this boat.'

'I know what you mean,' Lee said ruefully.

Chi, deep in her memory, continued as if he had not spoken. 'Then it grew hot and airless and although it was very dark I felt I could see the sides moving in towards me, pressing against my feet. I found a chink of light coming through a crack near the bottom of the door and I pressed my eye to it. I can still feel the draught of cold air on my eye-ball. But all the time I was worried that the sides of the cupboard were going to press in on me. When my parents came back they heard me moaning and when they opened the door they found me pressing the sides out as hard as I could with hands and feet. At first they thought I was trying to get out until I told them I didn't want to be crushed to death.' Chi sucked her bottom lip for a moment. 'Do you know, they told me afterwards, they'd only been gone an hour, to me it seemed like days!'

The boat lifted and fell gently in the slight breeze. The only noise apart from the engine came from Trinh and grandfather as they worked at the mast. Lee changed hands, rubbed an aching wrist against his knee.

'It must have been awful for you down there,' he said eventually.

'Not as bad as it was for Lan and Khai. If it had not been for your grandfather what happened to Lan could have happened to me. How can people do things like that to people?'

She turned to look directly at Lee as she asked the question and although he was aware of her eyes on him he could not bring himself to meet them.

'They did in the war,' he said with a shrug.

'In a war people can find excuses. They do things for what they believe in, out of fear, all kinds of reasons which I might not agree with but I can understand. What those men did was out of pure, brutal greed. They didn't have to do those things to rob us. They could have taken what gold they wanted without that.' She fell silent for a moment. 'Kim said you were very brave.'

Lee couldn't help smiling. 'All I did was lose our water bottles.'

'Your grandfather said it wasn't your fault.'

'I should at least have thrown some of our empty water bottles back. That way we would have been able to collect water again if it rains. I should have done something instead of standing there helpless.'

'What could you have done?'

'I don't know. Fought with the man who was holding me, cut the two boats adrift, anything would have been better than nothing.'

'If you'd done anything like that you'd probably have got yourself killed,' Chi pointed out.

'In the end I was too frightened to jump, let alone *do* anything.'

'Did you cry?'

'Not until it was over and I was back on this boat.'

'There you are then. Being brave isn't being stupid, it's doing everything you can do in the circumstances and you did that.'

Lee nodded but remained unconvinced. 'When I knew we were going to leave on this boat I thought it was going to be a tremendous adventure.'

'It has been,' Chi said bitterly twisting her long delicate fingers together.

'But not the way I thought.'

'I was frightened from the very beginning,' Chi admitted, 'and I still am. I've never trusted the sea.'

'I didn't realise that,' Lee said, startled by her confession. 'You always seem so calm about it all.' Chi shrugged. Lee remembered the words his father kept on using lately. 'At least we're free this way.'

'Free? Yes, free to drown or die of thirst or hunger. Chi looked round bleakly. 'What a place!'

Lee just managed to stop himself touching Chi to try and comfort her. 'Don't worry, we'll make it, I'm sure.'

As if to confirm his words a cheer went up as grandfather and Trinh hoisted the new, rough mast up on to the cabin-top.

'Soon we'll have a sail, that'll make things safer,' Lee added.

94

Chi nodded silently and left him. As he watched her go, he realised he had told her things he had not and could not tell anybody else. He even had to admit that he no longer looked upon her as a nuisance, though he was loath to admit that even to himself.

The sail was hoisted and the engine switched off in order to save oil and fuel. The quiet felt unreal.

Trinh came to relieve Lee. His eyes ached from the constant glare of the sea, his tongue was heavy and swollen from the heat and thirst. He sat on the deck next to his mother and fell into an instant, deep sleep.

Next day they were still moving under sail. It would always be used now when ever there was the slightest breath of favourable wind. As people woke they took it in turns to stand up and stretch their cramped limbs and strain their eyes to catch the first glimpse of land but there was none to see.

During the day the wind died away altogether and Trinh was forced to restart the engine and everyone watched anxiously as he made frequent trips back and forth to check the oil levels. They fell asleep to the sound of the engine. In the past that had been a comforting sound but now they knew the engine could not run without oil and the oil was fast running out.

It was still dark when Lee woke, sweating with fear, from an extended version of his usual nightmare in which one of his hands was now trapped between the two boats and it was slowly being crushed to a pulp. He tried to wriggle down into his blanket and get back to sleep but couldn't. Then he heard Trinh padding along the gunwale and saw his shadowy figure disappear into the engine-room. Lee, with his orange and brown blanket still round his shoulders for the night was cool now he was fully awake, went to join him.

Trinh was just coming up the steps. 'Very little oil left in her now,' he said, shaking his head. 'If there isn't a wind soon we'll have to stop the engine anyway or risk doing it serious damage.'

He made his way back to the tiller and left Lee squatting on the top step gazing out into the darkness listening to the drum of the engine and the sound of the water.

'Can't you sleep either?' Chi's voice whispered at his elbow.

'No.' He didn't want to talk about the nightmare.

Chi shivered a little.

'Do you want a bit of my blanket?' he asked, hoping she would say no but she nodded. He held one side up and she snuggled under it. Her hair brushed his face and it made him feel uncomfortable. 'I've got a stick of gum. Would you like it?' Again she nodded and he used looking for the chewing gum as an excuse to push the blanket off and move away from her. He'd kept the gum in the pocket of his jeans ever since they'd boarded the boat because he knew that once he had eaten it he'd only crave more and there was no way he would be able to get any. Reluctantly he handed it over.

'Thanks,' Chi said, then she broke the stick and handed half back.

'Oh, thanks,' Lee said carelessly. 'I'll eat mine later if you don't mind.' Then he stuffed it back deep into his pocket. He didn't want to have to cope with a craving for chewing gum on top of everything else. He made a firm resolution not to touch it until they reached Hong Kong. He'd noticed how much the smokers who'd run out of cigarettes were suffering.

Even so he had to try not to think about it while Chi was chewing but his tongue was longing for the sugary sweetness, and he was on the point of asking her to go and eat it somewhere else when she leant across and whispered something to him.

Her long hair brushed his face again and he missed what she'd said. 'What did you say?'

Chi repeated it, a little louder this time. 'Phan, the baby is dead.'

Lee couldn't believe her. 'Your mother's still holding him.'

'I know, but he died this afternoon. She won't let go of him. She keeps hugging him and singing to him as if he were still alive.'

He thought the whole thing sounded a little creepy and unreal. 'Can't your father do anything?'

'My mother's threatened to jump overboard if he does anything to the baby. She says he's only sleeping.'

TWELVE

'Check the oil, Lee,' grandfather said wearily.

As Lee pulled the thin rod out, wiped it on some cotton waste and dipped it in again, he couldn't get out of his mind the figure of Hue, hunched over her baby so that neither of their faces could be seen while she crooned to it. He was certain he should tell somebody and the engine-room was the only place he wasn't likely to be overheard.

'There's very little left,' he said as he checked the thick black line which was well below the danger level.

'What about kerosene?'

Lee checked that too. 'Not much left.'

'It seems to me, with no wind, we might just as well use the kerosene up in the hope we reach land,' the old man said thoughtfully.

'The engine would seize up. It might wreck the piston,' Lee pointed out.

'If we haven't any kerosene and we haven't reached land, it won't matter whether the engine seizes up or not. We might reach land before dark if we do use it, on the other hand.'

One of the things which was frightening them all was that they would pass land and not know it because it would happen under the cover of darkness. Only last night, while Lee was still trying to get to sleep, the forward watch had shouted out he could see lights. Everyone had woken up to look but it had turned out to be a ship in the distance, unaware of their existence. Nevertheless the fear was very real and grandfather always felt it was more important to cover more distance during daylight than it was at night.

'Start the engine,' he said and Lee swung the handle. It spluttered into life and grandfather was just about to climb up on deck when Lee called him back. 'Grandfather, I need to share a secret.'

'Is it a good secret or a bad one?'

'A bad one.'

'There are some things I would rather not know. Think hard before you tell me this one.'

'I have and this is so frightening I need to share it although I promised Chi I wouldn't tell anybody.'

'Is it about Chi? Or her mother?'

'Her mother,' Lee admitted, surprised that grandfather seemed to know already what he was going to say.

'And the baby, Phan? I thought as much. You don't have to worry about telling me that because your mother already has. She knew because she's taken over the nursing from Lan and when she talked to Hue yesterday she could see the baby was dead.'

'What are you going to do? This morning Hue was still rocking him and singing to him as if he was still alive.'

'Poor Hue,' the old man said, 'to lose Quan was bad enough but now Phan as well!' The old man shook his head slowly. 'The baby must have a sea burial as soon as possible otherwise in this heat all of us could be in danger. Lee, don't mention this to anyone. You've seen how easily people can panic. I'll think of something.' He clapped a hand on Lee's shoulder. 'I hope all this is going to be worth it, these are awful things for a child to see.'

'I'm not a child any more, grandfather,' Lee protested but grandfather had clambered up on to the deck and didn't hear him.

Reluctantly Lee went and sat with the rest of the family but he kept his back to Hue because the sight was too awful. He found it impossible to connect Hue as she was now with the woman with the round smiling face he'd first met.

Lee had no appetite for the midday meal and he kept wanting to tell Tam, who was particularly lively, to shut up but he knew he couldn't. He was almost relieved when the engine faltered and died and grandfather laid aside his chopsticks, asking Lee to come and help.

'There's still a little kerosene left,' Lee confirmed, 'but not enough oil to show on the dipstick and the engine's very hot.'

'Try and start her.'

Lee swung the handle but the engine refused to start. He tried again with same result. 'There are several things it could be. I mean we're pretty low in the fuel tank so a certain amount of muck is being dredged up. It could just be a blocked jet.'

'Try everything,' grandfather said, 'even if only to keep people's minds from the truth for as long as possible. And anyway you might be lucky. Start stripping it down while I go and tell Trinh the truth.'

Nothing could have pleased Lee more, he opened the tool box and set to work straight away, trying hard to remember everything he'd learnt during the furtive sessions at the garage.

By the time grandfather got back Lee held the cause of the trouble in the palm of his oil-stained hands.

'It's the piston. The oil dried up, the engine overheated and it's cracked the piston.'

'There's nothing we can do about that!'

'Not without a new piston,' Lee agreed, 'and even then the engine won't work if the broken one has damaged the valve.'

As they clambered up there wasn't a breath of air and the sail hung limply above them. Trinh was sculling just to keep her moving at all but it was obvious he couldn't keep that up for long, and in any case they were making very little headway.

While the boat had been under way it had created its own slight breeze but now it was stationary under the heat of the afternoon sun. There was not a cloud in the sky. Several tried tipping sea-water over themselves and allowing the sun to evaporate it, which had a temporary cooling effect. But when Lee tried it, he found the effect wore off very quickly and the salt the water left behind was an additional irritant to the abscesses which had spread to his legs.

'We must rig as many shelters as we can,' Trinh suggested. They did this using blankets, plastic bags, anything they could lay hands on, and although lying beneath it was shady it was still hot and airless.

'Perhaps we ought to climb under the deck like the girls did,' someone suggested.

'If anybody does,' Lee's father piped up, 'perhaps they would get my watch back.'

In the hurry to get the girls out and the shock of what had happened to Lan and Khai, the box of valuables had been completely forgotten.

'I'll get the hammer,' father said, and everybody gathered round to watch as he pulled up the planks because at least for half-an-hour it would provide a slight diversion from their danger and discomfort. As soon as the planks were up father waved towards the hole. 'Come on, Lee. You get them out.'

The stench of the bilge-water brought memories back to all of them and as Lee climbed down he couldn't help remembering Chi's story about being shut in the cupboard. The box had slipped further under than he'd expected and he had a very uncomfortable crawl on his belly through the filthy water to retrieve it. Having reached it, getting back wasn't easy because the cardboard was disintegrating in the damp.

On the way back his eyes had grown a little more accustomed to the small amount of light which filtered down through cracks in the deck and he noticed a damp patch on the side planks, clear of the bilges.

When he moved over to investigate he discovered water seeping quite freely between the planks just as it had above the deck. Having found one patch he looked for others despite anxious voices calling to him from above. He found one more, not quite as bad as the first but bad enough.

He handed the box up. It dripped water back down on him. When he got out of the hole people were busy claiming their possessions, welcoming them like long-lost friends, hugging and even kissing them. Lee couldn't help thinking how odd it was that while their lives were in danger people should care so much for valuable but, at the moment, useless things.

Lee was more concerned with telling Trinh and grandfather about the leaks he'd discovered. 'I'll go and sluice myself off in the stern.'

'Don't forget your watch, Lee,' his father said holding it out to him.

'Thanks,' Lee said but as he strapped it on he thought how little use it was. Out here where a day could stretch into infinity it was sometimes better not to know the time.

Trinh was in the stern, more out of habit than any necessity as the boat was barely moving, and Lee was able to tell about the leaks he'd discovered as he sluiced off the stinking slime.

'They're well above the bilge water but below the waterline,' Lee explained. 'One on each side, one half way along, the other quite near the front.'

'Thanks for telling me. Now the engine isn't working we'll have to bale by hand and with those leaks it'll be even more important.'

'Can you patch her?'

'Not while she's in the water. We could if we could beach her. There may be more in the stern beneath us. She's an old boat but the best I could get and I thought she'd get us to Hong Kong for her last voyage.'

Lee was about to leave Trinh to his troubles when he caught sight of something he thought was land on the horizon. He was about to say so when he realised it was a ship.

'Look, Trinh, out there! There's a ship heading this way.'

Others heard his cry and rushed to the side of the boat shouting and waving to attract the attention of the ship which was steaming steadily towards them. They shouted for food, for water, for help, for anything. They waved clothing and plastic bags but the closer the ship got the clearer it was that it would neither alter course, nor slacken speed.

'They're not going to stop,' Lee gasped.

'No, I don't believe they are,' Trinh said.

The people on the fishing-boat were screaming their lungs out, their hands outstretched towards the rusty old cargo boat as if they were begging for alms. A couple of men walking by the ship's rail waved cheerily as if the fishing-boat were on a pleasure cruise. The man at the helm blew a couple of derisive hoots on the ship's siren.

Some of the refugees collapsed to the deck in tears. They had truly believed that help was at hand.

'It is the law of the sea,' Trinh said bitterly, 'that every captain must help anyone in distress.'

As Lee watched, a man walked to the rail and tossed over a basket full of refuse from the ship's galley. It fell to the sea in multi-coloured confusion.

As the stern swept past the fishing-boat setting it bobbing like a cork, a man stopped taking photographs of his shipmates to take pictures of the anguished, up-turned faces of the refugees.

'Why won't they help?'

'Some do, most don't. If they arrive in port with refugees on board it would mean trouble with immigration and delay for their cargo and their ship. That makes the ship's owners, most of whom have never been to sea except for a cruise, very angry. So angry it spoils the meals they eat at their overloaded tables while we just die,' Trinh said.

'They could have given us food or water.'

'I suppose they could. But why us? Why not any one of the hundred or so boats like ours they pass on every journey through these waters. No, Lee, I'm afraid Vietnamese refugees are a common sight out here. Still, let's go and see what they did leave us.' Trinh picked up the oar and slowly sculled the boat across to where the refuse the man had thrown overboard was floating amongst the rainbow stain of oil the ship had discharged out of her bilges.

As they drew near, eager hands scrabbled amongst the rubbish that remained. Lee felt sick as he watched people lifting out and eating the rotting vegetables and mouldy loaves, the ship's cook had rejected. One man found a cigarette packet with a single cigarette still in it but threw it away in dismay when he discovered it was wet and ruined, only to see it fought over by two other men who thought it might still be salvaged.

'This is what we have sunk to!' Trinh said shaking his head sadly. 'Dogs fighting over scraps.'

That night a wind sprang up. The sail was hoisted and Trinh was a changed man, grinning with excitement as he urged the boat through the water.

'Take it easy, Trinh,' grandfather cautioned, 'remember that isn't a proper mast and we can't afford to lose it.'

'We can't afford to waste a favourable wind either, ' Trinh replied, the wind streaming through his hair.

'Drop the sail, before we lose it.'

As he spoke there was a creaking crash as sail and mast were carried overboard to be swallowed up by the darkness.

'What happens now?' Lee asked, shivering as the boat was helplessly tossed in the howling gale.

'You pray that the wind we wanted so much goes away again as quickly as possible. And in the meantime bale as hard as you can!'

No longer able to control the boat at all, waves kept crashing over her. With no engine and therefore no bilge-pump there was nothing to do but bale with everything they could find again. They continued to bale all night. They only paused to be sick over the side, if they could manage it. Their hands were bloody and bruised where they caught the woodwork but somehow they managed to keep the water level down and the boat afloat despite the creaks and protestations of her timbers.

As dawn came, the wind began to ease and those still baling were glad to slump down onto the deck wherever they stood. Some fell asleep where they sat on the soaking-wet deck but they leapt to their feet as Trinh shouted at the top of his voice, 'Land!'

Lee couldn't believe his ears and stood up to see for himself. Only a short distance away a small, steep-sided island rose almost sheer out of the water which crashed on to its narrow beaches. Although there were no houses on this side of the island, it seemed perfectly possible there might be on the far side. Even if there were none at least they would be safe from the elements for a while.

All over the boat people laughed, cried and hugged each other. Tam and some of the other small children danced up and down with excitement. Then Tam drew away from them, came up beside her mother and tugged at her clothing.

'Will there be dragons on the island?' she asked with huge round eyes.

Everyone who heard laughed but Tam was perfectly serious about it.

'I shouldn't think so,' mother said with a smile.

'Can you get her in?' grandfather asked sternly. He was taking no part in the jubilation for he saw how steeply the great rock rose out of the water and a strong sea was driving them so hard towards it they could be smashed to pieces.

'I think so,' Trinh said through gritted teeth. He too had seen the danger but he'd chosen his spot, as best he could, a sandy bay, though with jagged rocks on either side.

The boat fell silent as they all realised the danger they were still in and grandfather urged them all to sit down out of the way. Lee could feel the strong waves lifting the boat and carrying it in towards the shore. He could also hear the surf crashing over the rocks. What he could not see was where the boat was pointing but he knew full well that those rocks could rip their small boat to pieces.

Lee heard grandfather shout, 'Look out!'

There was a dreadful crunching sound followed by a dull thud as the bottom of the boat struck the jagged edge of a submerged rock. It jolted the boat so badly its passengers were thrown across the deck. Lee expected to hear the boat begin to break up until he felt another wave lift them high in the air then it dropped with a sickening crash and came to a juddering, scrunching halt.

'We've done it!' grandfather cried out.

Everybody picked themselves up rubbing their bruises. The boat had been set down neatly in shallow water in the centre of the bay. There were whoops and shouts as people swarmed over the side, dropped into the shallow water and splashed up to the beach. Once there, some fell on to their knees with tears in their eyes and kissed the sand. Most had never expected to stand on solid ground again.

Lee turned back to look at the boat which in the end had brought them there safely. It was then that he saw grandfather with Hue wading out into deeper water. They didn't stop until it reached their chests. Grandfather gently took the dead baby from her arms and let it float away on the water.

Lee expected to see it swept back towards the shore but he hadn't reckoned with grandfather's skill and experience. He was using the same cross-current that had thrown the boat on to the rock and it drew the baby away from them now.

Hue let out a howl of anguish as she threw herself after it but grandfather held her fast until she quietened, then they both turned and waded back to the shore where Minh and Chi waited in silence.

Even now Lee expected to see the tiny figure of the baby caught up on the rocks, rejected by the sea which had played its part in taking Phan's life. It looked almost like a sacrifice or offering for their deliverance as it floated on the water.

As it neared the rocks Lee held his breath but he needn't have worried. The baby floated off, accepted by the sea, like a small white flower.

THIRTEEN

'I can't stand up,' Tam giggled as she collapsed into the sand.

Others had the same problem. After days and nights of constant motion desperately seeking dry land, now they had found it they couldn't stand up on it. Solid ground seemed to sway as much as the boat had. The muscles of some of the older passengers were so stiff these poor people had to be carried ashore.

Another thing which took them by surprise was their fear of space. They had grown so used to the cramped quarters on the boat that having tasted the freedom the beach offered, they all sat close to each other in an area only slightly larger than the boat allowed.

But they still looked round their new surroundings with interest. Lee was looking forward to climbing up the massive hill, thinly-clad with shrivelled grass and stunted bushes, which rose sharply from the narrow beach.

'I'd feel happier if there was any sign of habitation,' father said quietly.

'Perhaps they live on the other side of the island,' mother said, busy treating minor cuts and bruises which some of the passengers sustained as the boat beached itself. 'I'm just thankful we've found land at all. There were times when I thought last night might be our last.'

'The first thing we must do,' grandfather announced, 'is get the boat properly beached as the tide goes out. If you can all collect everything you need off her first and then the men can help Trinh and me.'

After the boat was unloaded the men drove stakes, again salvaged from the wreck, deep into the sand. These were lashed to the sides of the boat so that when the tide went out it was held upright as the keel settled into the sand.

As the tide ebbed, the damage done by the rock as they came in to land was clearly visible. There was a great gash of newly-splintered wood where it had hit and only the thickness of the wood had stopped her being holed.

Equally obvious were the leaks which Lee had found with such difficulty and, just as Trinh had feared, there were more in the stern section.

Grandfather was busy melting a lump of tar, which they had brought with them in a pot, over a driftwood fire. Trinh was fraying an old rope with which to caulk the cracks.

'Can I go and explore?' Lee asked his father.

'I don't see why not, but keep in sight.'

'I want to go too,' Kim said getting to her feet.

'And me,' Tam jumped up, more certain on her feet now than she had been at first.

All three of them ran up the beach. 'I'll race you to the top of the hill,' he shouted, his father's cautious words forgotten. But very quickly he ran out of breath and his legs went weak.

'Wait, not so fast!' Kim called out as she struggled along with Tam.

The lack of exercise while they'd been on the boat, together with their poor diet, had left them in no condition for hill climbing.

'We're out of practice,' Lee grinned and they altered the line of their walk so that they walked along the hill instead of up it. Even so the rough ground was heavy going and they made frequent stops every few metres while they pretended to admire the view.

Looking ahead of them Lee could see a little cleft in the hillside where the grass looked less brown and as they drew near he saw why.

'There's water coming out of the side of the hill,' he shouted.

His words carried across the hillside and people down

on the beach caught them and passed them on to their neighbours, some of whom were already running towards Lee, clutching bowls or cooking pots.

Out of the rock came a stream of sparkling, clear water, which had created a natural bowl in the rock where it fell. From the bowl the overflow splashed down the hillside to run across a beach and into the sea just beyond the jagged rocks, which was why they hadn't noticed it until now.

Lee dropped to his knees beside the natural bowl, cupped his hand and tasted what seemed the best water he'd ever drunk. Pure, fresh and very cold as it ran straight from the rock, he could feel it soothing his parched gullet and trace its icy advance as it ran towards his stomach.

He'd savoured the first mouthful but then he greedily drank mouthful after mouthful, splashing it over his face and hair, letting it drip from his chin.

Tam nudged past him and held her head upside down to let the water run directly into her mouth in a steady jet.

Kim put her hot bare feet below the bowl and squirmed with delight as the cold water ran over them.

By now others were pushing past them to drink the water from the source but many more had found the line of the stream further down and were standing fully-clothed in it, tipping the water over themselves to wash the salt from their clothing and their bodies.

Lee had drunk so much, his belly felt bloated and as he walked back to the beach, hand in hand with Kim and Tam, he thought he could hear the water slushing about inside him.

At the head of the beach a little old man had built a shrine with stones he'd gathered and, when the midday meal was ready, people placed small helpings of food in front of it as a way of offering thanks for their escape from death.

Hue, Minh, and Chi didn't, they sat apart from the

others, Hue had cried for most of the morning.

As the perfume of incense mingled with the smell of food and grandfather's tar, everybody seemed more relaxed but grandfather was determined they shouldn't grow complacent.

'Remember, we're stranded on an island with no fuel or oil and an engine which doesn't work. We've lost our mast and sail. The food we have may run out any day, which would leave us with only the fish we can catch. We must look for help straight away.'

'While you and Trinh work on the boat I'll lead a party round the island to try and find help,' father suggested and grandfather nodded in agreement. 'I think it would be better to go round because that way we can't get lost as we're bound to end up back here eventually. Also it will make the going fairly level.' Several men offered to go with him and then father turned to Lee. 'Are you coming or not, Lee?'

Lee shook his head. He had other plans. He waited until the men had left and the women were beating their washing on the stones by the stream and then he set off up the hill. He was determined it would not defeat him again. This time he set out at a steady pace, planning to take rests whenever he needed them, but he would make it to the top simply because he wanted to be the first to bring back the good news of what lay on the other side.

The afternoon sun was hot. There were no trees for shade, the only vegetation was the brown stunted grass. Most of the steep hill was rock which in places had been eroded into sand by the extremely severe climate. The only company was an occasional bird and two butterflies but that didn't bother Lee. The feeling of space suddenly felt luxurious.

His fifth stop was high on the shoulder of the hill. There he found a rock which offered a little shade and a support for his tired back while he massaged his aching legs. He could still hear the thump, thump of grandfather's hammer.

The boat looked no larger than a piece of driftwood, it seemed impossible it could ever have contained the lives of forty people. He heard the shouts of the children as they chased each other along the beach, though he noticed that none dared go into the sea.

Way over to the left, he could see the little knot of men his father was leading as they made their way round the beach. Spurred on by the thought that he'd know the lie of the land sooner than they, he hauled himself to his feet and scrambled up the last few metres to the summit, where he sank exhausted to the ground. The breeze lifted his hair slightly as he looked round, unable to believe what he saw. They had landed on a totally uninhabited island. Tears of anger and frustration rolled down his cheeks. He kicked savagely at a stone which went careering down the deserted hillside.

He took his time descending. He was no longer anxious to be the first back with the news. He stopped for a long time by the spring, knowing now that it was the only blessing the island had to bestow on them, drinking the cold water and sluicing it round his head. He stayed until he saw his father lead the men back onto the beach from their fruitless circuit and then he joined them soon after they had told Trinh and grandfather the bad news.

'I'm not that surprised,' grandfather grunted at them as he pressed string, fat with the black tar, into one of the cracks in the side of the boat.

'When you've finished the repairs,' father said as he mopped his brow, 'we could try to find another island which might have people on it who could help us.'

'I climbed to the top of the hill,' Lee put in, 'I couldn't see another island in any direction.'

'That doesn't mean there isn't one,' Trinh said without much hope in his voice. 'I'll climb up after dark, I may be able to see some lights.'

'I think we ought to build a beacon before nightfall,' grandfather suggested. 'We don't have any distress flares, they aren't the kind of thing you can buy on the black market, but it would be a pity if a ship went past without seeing us. Collect all the driftwood you can find on the beach and pile it up. It can go up the hill tomorrow.'

'Keep a special look out for anything that would make a mast,' Trinh added.

They all eagerly fanned out across the beach and began to collect every scrap of wood, no matter how small, they could find. The children joined in too for a while but soon lost interest and went back to their games.

That night they all slept on the beach except for Trinh, who insisted on sleeping on the boat. 'If a storm blew up and that floated off we really would be in a mess.'

As soon as the sun rose, but before the heat of the day set in, they set about the gruelling task of getting the wood they had collected up to the top of the hill. They organised a chain of people up the steep path so that nobody had to walk too far but merely transferred as much as they could comfortably carry.

Lee helped with the carrying but most of the children either just ran about or sometimes took up buckets of water from the cool spring from which the men drank.

Chi was the other exception. She insisted on helping with the work and was assigned to the section just below Lee. Consequently they sometimes met, although Lee was too shy to actually take wood from her arms and always collected it from the pile on the ground. But they did sometimes pause for breath from which Lee quickly gathered that Chi had really volunteered to be free for a time from the oppressive sadness of her parents.

'Mother's done little else but cry since we landed,' Chi said when she stopped to scoop up water with her hand from the bucket Tam offered.

'I suppose you can't expect anything else,' Lee mumbled. He didn't really know what to say but it was the sort of thing he'd heard his parents saying about Hue and Minh.

'But I wish they would let me share their grief,' Chi said quietly. 'It's as if it's something so very private that I can take no part in it, as if I'm not part of the family. I loved Phan too, nobody was more pleased than me when he was born. I love babies and him especially. I helped bath him and I often used to sit with mother and sing him to sleep. But now they've forgotten all that and they've cut themselves off from me completely.'

Lee was saved from having to answer by a shout which came from further up the hill asking for more wood as they'd run out.

By the time the sun was high enough in the sky to make further work impossible they had quite a respectable pile at the top of the hill and were all glad to go down to the beach to find what little shade they could amongst the rocks or impromptu shelters people had put up. Two men stayed up at the top to keep watch for any passing ships using the same rota that had been used for watches on board their boat.

They had strict instructions only to light the beacon when they were sure a ship or boat could really see it.

'If it's coming towards us, or on a course which will take it quite close to us, wait until the last possible minute before lighting it,' Trinh advised.

'What about aeroplanes?' Hung asked.

'Only if they're quite close and low-flying,' grandfather said firmly.

'Helicopters and light planes,' added Trinh, 'I doubt if an airliner bound for America would notice us, or bother much if it did.'

Lee, not being due on watch until the following day with Hung, decided to wander off along the beach on his own but he'd only gone a short distance before he looked round and saw Chi following him. At least she wasn't actually following him but if they both kept on walking at the same speed their paths were sure to cross at the same moment!

When they met she said, 'Let's run.' She took off, her bare feet flicking sand as she fled across the flat sand, her long hair streaming out behind her. Determined not to be beaten Lee chased after her but couldn't catch her before they reached the promontory of jagged rocks which blocked their way.

'You're crazy!' Lee said as he flopped down beside her.

'It just feels so wonderful to be on land again,' she said, gasping for breath, 'and have all this space to move about in.'

She got up again almost straight away and Lee thought she was about to run back but this time she ran towards the sea. As she was fully clothed the thought crossed his mind that she was about to try and drown herself. She ran in until she was waist deep. Lee rose to follow her. She ducked her head beneath the waves and Lee expected to see her floating off like her little baby brother, but the next moment she was walking back towards him, water streaming from her black trousers and blouse, wet strands of hair on her shoulders.

'Now I know you are crazy!'

'I'm not frightened of the sea now that I'm not on it any more.' She sank back on to the sand. 'I don't mind how long we have to stay on the island. Anything would be better than getting back on that boat.'

'Until the food runs out,' Lee suggested.

'Even then I would far rather die on land than at sea,' Chi said after some serious consideration. 'I wish Phan had been buried on the island instead of at sea, he had no reason to love it either.'

Lee turned to look at Chi and saw tears welling up in her eyes to join the sea-water which trickled down her cheeks. He was at a loss to know what to do. When Tam cried about a broken toy or a hurt knee she was soon comforted. Chi's crying was different and what made it more disturbing was that it was done absolutely silently.

'I am sorry about Phan,' was the best he could manage.

'I'm not crying for Phan. He's dead and out of it all. I'm crying for the rest of us: for my parents, for everything!'

She got up and stamped away from Lee. He let her go, got up and wandered off in the opposite direction kicking at the sand as he went. His foot caught against something that looked like wood and remembering the beacon he knelt down to clear the sand with his hands like a dog. When he'd finished he had a pole about three metres long which had been washed ashore by the sea and painstakingly buried by successive tides. Despite being a little rough it was very sturdy.

A shadow fell across it and he looked up to find Chi standing beside him.

'I'm sorry for being so stupid,' she said quietly.

He shrugged her apology off. 'Look what I've found. This would make a new mast for the boat.'

'I suppose it would.'

'Help me carry it back,' he said, although he could have managed it perfectly well on his own.

Lee felt he detected a certain reluctance on her part to do anything which would hasten their departure but she did help him.

When they saw it grandfather and Trinh were much more pleased with Lee's find.

'All we need now is a sail,' Trinh said as they hauled the pole on board and measured it against the engine-cabin.

'If the wind wasn't too strong we could use something like a blanket until we can get a proper sail,' grandfather said. 'Even so, I wouldn't like to put to sea with only that for power unless there was a good chance of finding land fairly quickly, or at least another boat.'

During their midday meal Lee noticed that people were beginning to spread out a little more along the beach as they grew used to the space it offered. The

116

North Vietnamese were furthest away, but each family had its own little encampment except that Hue, Minh and Chi had moved up close to Lee's family.

Grandmother seemed to be looking after them, offering them food and talking quietly to Hue, who had at last stopped crying though her eyes were still red-rimmed and she spoke little. Lee felt embarrassed to have Chi sitting so close and didn't like to speak to her in front of the rest of the family. While he and Tam were washing out their rice-bowls in the stream she said, 'It must be nice to have your girl-friend with us.'

'She isn't my girl-friend,' Lee said and tried to scowl at Tam but only ended up blushing.

'You spend more time with her than you do with me anyway,' Tam retorted.

'That's because you are so silly,' Lee said angrily but he made sure he went with grandfather that afternoon when he said he was going fishing off the end of the rocks.

'Why haven't you brought bait and lines?' Lee asked when they sat down on the end of the promontory where there was quite deep water.

'I've got a few grains of rice here,' grandfather said opening his hand to show Lee. 'With this, if you sit very still for a moment, I should be able to catch as many fish as we need.'

'But you haven't got a line,' Lee insisted.

'No, today I shall catch my line, bait and fish. Watch!'

Grandfather pulled a sling from his pocket, selected a stone and fitted it into the sling. Seconds later the sling whipped round, the stone zipped through the air and a stunned gull plummeted to the rock.

The old man pounced on the bird, 'Lend me your knife again,' he said.

Lee watched with very mixed emotions as grandfather plunged the knife into the bird's body and the white breast feathers turned red with its own still-warm blood. He knew that if they were to survive, other creatures had to die and be used as food. He had never minded about the countless fish he'd eaten, but it saddened him to see this great bird which had only moments ago been flying around them, a free spirit, lying dead and bloody on the ground.

Grandfather's attitude was practical and businesslike as ever. He cut off the great wings, soaked one in the blood, which seeped from the dismembered body, and plunged it into the sea.

Shadows darted quickly towards it. Grandfather flicked his wrist and to Lee's astonishment three quite large fish, hooked by the feathers as they attempted to suck out the blood, landed on the rock beside them.

In a very short time they had enough fish to feed them all amply. Not only that but grandmother plucked the dead bird and chopped it up for their evening meal, but Lee couldn't bring himself to eat any of it and was secretly pleased when Kim and Tam said it was too oily.

Nobody on watch at the top of the hill reported anything during that day, and throughout the night the only sighting was of distant lights, which might have belonged to a cargo boat, but they had been so far off the men had decided they wouldn't waste the beacon.

But that afternoon a ship was clearly spotted heading due east. The beacon was lit. As the dry timber caught sparks flew up into the air ahead of the bright yellow flames.

'I knew there would be dragons here,' Tam said as she watched the fire, 'they live in a nest at the top of the hill.'

But nobody heard her. Most people ran down to the water's edge to shout and cheer but if the helmsman noticed them there was no sign. The ship did not alter course and eventually dropped out of sight over the horizon. There was nothing left to do but start the onerous task of building another beacon.

Since they had landed, every scrap of wood in the

immediate area had been burnt either on the cooking-fires or the beacon. Consequently wood had to be dragged back from further afield as well as hauled up the steep slope.

Hung and Lee took up their positions beside the new beacon just as the sun was setting.

'Look!' Lee pointed out to sea where a vessel was just coming into sight. 'It's heading almost straight for us.'

'You're right! Don't light the beacon until she's on top of us.'

Hardly able to contain their excitement they watched the ship plough steadily through the water. Hung had the matches in his hand ready to strike.

'Now,' Hung said and struck the match.

The dried grass at the beacon's base spluttered into yellow flame, the dry timber above crackled into life and a glow of light lit their excited faces and the whole hillside.

Seeing the beacon lit again, the people on the beach shouted and waved through the twilight although it was doubtful that they could be seen or heard.

Up at the top of hill Hung had stripped off his sweater and was waving it slowly between the ship and the fire to make it more noticeable but the ship carried on at a steady pace until it disappeared round the island.

'It was so close, it must have seen us!' Lee said bitterly through the gathering gloom now that all that was left of their fire were the glowing ashes.

'Maybe they did, but we're getting used to people who don't want to help.' Then Hung peered out to sea. 'There's another ship!'

'But we've nothing to burn.'

'Get anything you can that will burn. Quick.'

The two of them stumbled about in the dark, pulling up tufts of grass and the smallest twig which had been dropped during the preparation of the beacon. Anything they found was thrown into the hot embers. Some caught and burst into flame, some didn't, but either way the flames were too small to be noticeable and as Hung and Lee trudged gloomily down the hill the ship's engines became a distant rumble. With nothing left to burn, there was little point in keeping watch for the rest of the night.

About half way down they met a group of men toiling up towards them, carrying every scrap of wood they'd been able to gather together, and determined that there should a beacon on the hill at all times.

After the frustrating experience of Hung and Lee, it was decided that they should keep all spare wood at the top of the hill instead of at the bottom, and that in effect there should be two beacons so that there would always be a second chance.

'Ships often keep each other company,' grandfather explained.

But even if they had got the ground rules right they could not organise the weather and the next day the mist lay so thickly over the island there seemed little point in sending anybody up to the beacon.

Disheartened, they faced the fact they had enough rice for two more days. People wandered glumly about the beach trying hard to find things to do to pass the time.

Lee wandered down to their boat. Grandfather and Trinh were sitting on her deck whipping the ends of old frayed lines. He clambered up and squatted beside them, wondering if he would ever see this boat float again. The humid mist hung over them life a thick curtain and nobody bothered to speak.

Then Lee peered hard out to sea through the murk. 'I'm sure I can see a boat.'

Grandfather uncrossed his legs and stood up stiffly. 'I can't see anything.'

'Listen,' said Trinh.

They held their breath, heard nothing but the sea slopping up on the beach and then there was something else.

'It's an outboard-engine, quite close in,' said Trinh.

'Get a fire lit,' grandfather shouted, 'there's a boat out there in the mist!'

Because wood was in such short supply now, all the cooking-fires had died down. Feverish hands began to poke them back into life but it was obvious that the boat would have gone before they had flames of sufficient strength.

People were hollering for all they were worth from the beach but the man who sat hunched over his outboard-engine, intent on avoiding the rocks masked by the fog was hardly likely to hear them.

Lee whipped off his shirt, hung it in the struggling flames of one of the fires. Agonisingly slowly he watched it catch fire then he ran down the beach swirling it round his head like a flaming torch, shouting and calling as hard as he could.

Others followed suit. To their massive relief they heard the note of the boat's engine change as it slackened speed. Moments later they caught sight of its prow pushing through the thick mist towards them.

As it came nearer Lee couldn't help noticing the re-signed expression on Chi's face.

FOURTEEN

That night they tied up in a small fishing port on the coast of mainland China just east of Hainan. It was ironic that the island on which they were trapped was less than a day's sailing from safety. It was equally odd to Lee to be for the first time in a foreign country which was the home of his ancestors and whose language he spoke as well as he spoke Vietnamese.

The Chinese fisherman had accepted one gold digital watch, which he calculated would fetch a good price on the black market, as his fee for towing them home.

Glancing back at the island as it disappeared into the mist, like most of the other passengers, Lee felt a great sense of relief that they had been spared the slow agonising death from starvation which had faced them.

'I wish there had been dragons,' Tam said wistfully.

'No you don't,' Lee retorted. 'You'd have been scared silly.'

'Not if it was a baby dragon.'

With Minh and Hue sitting so close, the use of the word baby had even embarrassed Tam so she shut up. Chi, on the other hand, didn't look nearly so apprehensive about putting to sea again when she heard that it would be less than a day before they reached land.

As they entered the bustling little harbour it felt as if they had suddenly been thrown back into civilisation. Fishing-junks were easing their way round the crowded waters. Women with pigtails hanging from beneath their conical straw hats sculled sampans amongst them with a nonchalance that hid their skill and dexterity. The noise and bustle as they shouted back and forth to each other was intimidating to the refugees.

Even so, once they had been shown where to tie up for the night, Lee was anxious to climb the stone steps of the quay and explore his first foreign port. The only thing that stopped him was the slim figure of a soldier, who stood at the top of the steps clad in a greenish khaki uniform with red stars on the collar.

'Can we go ashore?' Lee eagerly asked his father.

'I think he's there to see we don't. Wait and see what Trinh has to say when he gets back from talking to the harbour-master.'

'Not until tomorrow,' Trinh explained when he returned. 'The officials who have to examine us and the boat have gone for the night and we must wait until they come back.'

But Lee needn't have worried. If he couldn't visit the town, the town was determined to visit him! Word had rapidly got about that another Vietnamese boat needing stores and provisions had docked. Whole families came down to the quay and while some stood and stared at the cramped boat full of foreigners, the majority brought cigarettes, fat hens and ducks as well as fresh vegetables.

At first the refugees weren't sure if the soldier, who was guarding them, would permit them to buy any of the goods.

'The only way to find out,' said grandfather, 'is to try. What do you want for that duck?'

'A watch,' said the farmer who had heard stories of how rich some of these refugees were.

'Two ducks for a watch,' grandfather said firmly.

The farmer shook his head at first but when grandfather shrugged and began to move away he changed his mind. 'All right,' he cried holding the ducks out.

Grandfather, with one eye on the soldier, climbed on to the cabin-roof and took them, handing over the watch in exchange.

The soldier took no notice and everybody else took that as a signal. Pandemonium broke out as transactions took place from all over the boat. The only time the soldier took any interest was when one seller got over-enthusiastic and climbed over the quay-rail to press his bargain. The soldier took a step forward and the crowd fell silent as it moved away from the edge, but seconds later they were back and the bartering continued.

Lee, Tam and Kim each had sticks of sugar cane from which they could suck the sticky sweetness once they had stripped the purple skin from it. Lee, realising Chi didn't have any, cut his stick in half with his pocket knife and gave her a piece.

It suddenly struck Lee that apart from the North Vietnamese who, speaking no Chinese, had had to be helped with their deals, Hue and Minh were the only people who had bought nothing. When he went with his mother to collect their rice ration he asked her why this was so.

'They have lost their will to live,' she explained. 'Losing Quan was bad enough but to have lost Phan as well has broken their spirit altogether.'

'But they still have a daughter,' Lee protested.

Mother smiled at him. 'You know that to the Chinese sons are always more highly-prized than daughters. Your father, who is much more liberal-minded than most, was very disappointed when Kim was our first-born but once we had you he didn't mind that our third child was a girl. Ideas change very slowly. Boys are lucky, bread-winners, girls are not. After all it isn't so very long since baby girls were thrown off the baby-tower and only kept in the unlikely event that they survived.'

'But that isn't fair on Chi.'

'Hue and Minh will get over all this eventually and have another son, then everything will be all right. Come on, we'll share our duck with them.'

The duck, which grandfather described as the most expensive meal he'd ever eaten in his entire life, was delicious after the endless fish and Lee couldn't help feeling a certain resentment that he had to share even one mouthful of it, even with Chi! But later that night he wished he'd given more away. He'd eaten so much he had a very bad stomach ache and he found it difficult to sleep.

Next day the effects of the rich food had not worn off and many people woke early from a poor night's sleep. Three straight-faced officials in blue jackets with red armbands, which bore gold ideograms, boarded the vessel and spent nearly an hour questioning Trinh in the stern of the boat. After that they talked briefly to all the adults and searched their possessions.

'Take up the boards,' the official in sunglasses said.

'There is only bilge-water and dirt under there,' grandfather replied.

'Take them up!'

Grandfather shrugged and got the hammer. The nails were drawn and one of the officials climbed down under the deck while the other two waited on deck.

As he waited, Lee remembered that he was not only in a foreign country but one which was unfriendly, if not actually at war, with the new Vietnamese government especially since they had started victimising the ethnic Chinese and forcing them to leave the country. But if the Chinese government didn't like the North Vietnamese they had been less friendly towards the Americans during the Vietnam war. Lee could not begin to understand how people could whip up so much hatred towards each other.

'There's nothing down there,' the man said as he climbed out of the hole.

Grandfather couldn't resist a smile at his smelly condition despite the boat being more water-tight since it had been repaired.

'You may stay here for today while you get the things you need for the next stage of your journey. The Republic of China welcomes you and wishes you well.'

'As long as we don't want to stay', father said quietly.

The man in sunglasses turned to look closely at Lee's father. 'We offer you every facility to obtain your objective. You must leave here at dawn tomorrow.' They all three turned to leave.

'It is all right for us to go ashore then?' Trinh wanted to be clear on that point.

'Of course,' the man said but he pointed at the North Vietnamese, 'except for those three.'

'They aren't spies, they're refugees too,' Lee's father put in firmly.

'Of course they aren't spies, but as they don't speak Chinese there would be little point in them going ashore, especially as they might get lost. They stay on board while you are here.'

'We need a new piston for our engine,' Trinh said. 'Do you know where we might get one?'

The officials shook their heads. 'Such things are difficult to get at short notice. They usually have to be ordered and often take weeks to get here.'

'Our engine is useless without it,' Trinh said.

'Then you'll have to manage with just a sail,' the official in sunglasses said in case they were thinking of using that as an excuse to stay longer than a day.

'The fisherman who towed us in thinks he might be able to find a spare sail but I would feel happier if we had an engine that worked,' Trinh said gloomily.

'I'm sorry I can't help you,' the man said and led the others off the boat.

Just as they reached the steps up to the quay, the one who had inspected the bilges, and who still smelled quite strongly, turned back and said quietly for Trinh's ears only, 'My uncle has a stall in the open market. Mostly he repairs bicycles but he does do the odd car or boat engine. You might try him.'

The man left before Trinh could thank him. The officials paused on the quay to have a brief word with the soldier who still stood on guard and then disappeared, leaving the refugees in no doubt that they would reappear if the boat did not leave on time the following day.

'Can we go now?' Lee hopped from foot to foot with

his impatience to get ashore.

'There are various things we need for the next stage of the voyage,' grandfather said. 'I suggest we split up into groups to make sure we have fuel, food and water before we leave.'

'You and I can go and look for the cycle man and see if we can get that piston or whatever it is,' Lee's father suggested.

Lee collected the old piston from the engine-cabin so that he could show the man what they wanted and they set out together. He was proud to be going with his father on a mission of some importance and relieved he didn't have to join Kim and Tam, who were going shopping with grandmother for food. Mother, who often didn't agree with her choice, had tactfully decided to remain on the boat and do some washing.

It wasn't difficult to find the way to the market. Everybody seemed to be moving in one direction. Cyclists, whose pillions were piled higher than themselves with goods, constantly rang their bells as they wove in and out amongst packed, dusty green buses which in turn honked at strange two-wheeled tractors dragging trailers at snail's pace towards the open market. It was Saturday when the people not only from the town but especially from the country districts enjoyed a day off. Most of the country people not only came to buy but also brought their own produce. They had raised it separately from the commune on their own private plots, and would sell it for the best price they could get.

Lee and his father flowed with the tide down narrow side-streets where second-hand clothing shops did a roaring trade but Lee glanced inside one or two other shops which had few customers and little to sell. In one a large glass display cabinet contained nothing but two tins of baby powder and if the shop had more to sell it was definitely under the counter.

Dust, flies and the smell of food hung in the air between the higgledy-piggledy, crumbling houses which-

flanked the street-market. Most of their ground floors were given over to open-fronted shops and every centimetre of pavement was filled with stalls and shoppers. The size of the stalls varied as much as the goods sold. Ducks advertised themselves from a cage in the gutter while the whole range of fruit and vegetables were piled high on a long trestle-table. Next to it a wizened old woman offered a few shrivelled oranges from a folding stool. The best cuts of meat and hanks of pink winddried sausages neatly laid-out on one stall were pressed up against a tray of offal crawling with bluebottles. Sacks of rice, bins of dried fruits, packets of spices, bamboo baskets of vegetables spilled off the stalls and on to the pavement.

An old man with strong nimble fingers sat on the pavement-edge mending saucepans, next to him another plundered an old wireless to get another working. The barber clipped the hair of a small boy who sat on a bamboo chair while his mother squatted patiently on a low three-legged stool.

The whole reminded Lee of the market back home in Cholon and yet he had an uneasy feeling all the time that he was being watched.

'That must be the stall,' his father said above the hubbub of bargaining. He was pointing towards a stall run by a thin man with a moustache who wore a cloth cap with a peak. 'We're looking for a part for our boat engine and one of the immigration officials, your nephew I think, said you might be able to help.'

The man didn't look up from the patch he'd just glued to an inner tube, which appeared to have had the same treatment each week for a number of years. 'Oh, yes?' he murmured as he dabbed chalk on to the patch to dry up the surplus glue.

'We need a new piston,' father persisted.

'Do you?' The man sounded so incredulous they might have asked for a space rocket but he still didn't look at them. Instead he handed the tube over to the-customer.

'Might you be able to help?' Father knew he had to keep his temper but Lee could tell he was getting testy.

'I might,' the man replied slowly as he concentrated on counting, three times, the money he'd just been paid.

'Show him what we want, Lee.'

Lee pulled out the newspaper parcel which contained the cracked piston.

'Don't get many of those,' the man said without looking at it. He broke off to haggle with a new customer over the price of a semi-bald, second-hand tyre. Only when the customer left, considering the price arrived-at too high, did the thin man turn all his attention to them.

'We're on our way to Hong Kong,' father began but he was interrupted straight away.

'I know where you're going and where you're from,' the man said, obviously already briefed by his nephew. 'Do you have any gold?'

'I don't,' father replied.

'But others amongst you have, you bring one *tael* here tonight at eight o'clock.' Lee was about to stuff the broken piston back in his pocket but the thin man took it from his hand. 'Leave that with me so that I can match it.'

'Thank you,' father said. 'You will be here at eight, it is very urgent, we have to leave first thing tomorrow.'

But they had lost his attention as new customers crowded round the stall.

As they walked away Lee couldn't help smiling when his father complained, 'I can't say I enjoy doing business with a shifty individual like that.'

Their next stop was at a letter writer's stall. His desk was covered with pens, inks and brushes while a canvas satchel, which hung from a nail in the brick pillar beside him, served as a stationery cupboard.

'I think we ought to send a letter to uncle Loc,' father said as he bought a pre-stamped airmail letter form. 'It hardly looks now as if we shall be returning and he could get on with the business of selling everything, if he hasn't already.'

While father wrote the letter Lee wandered across the street to a little stall covered with tiny items of jewellery. There were some small jade rings which Lee thought would look very beautiful on Chi's long delicate fingers. As he was admiring them his father came up behind him.

'What would you do with a ring?' he asked.

Lee blushed slightly. 'I just thought it might cheer Chi up a bit.'

'I'm sure it would,' father agreed, then his voice was more serious. 'Don't get too fond of Chi will you? In a few days' time we shall be in Hong Kong and you might never see her again. We might end up in different camps and eventually different countries. They might not want to go to America like us.'

'I'd just like to buy her something small, that's all.'

'Well, I'm afraid we can't as we don't have any money. All the gold, watches and everything else of value we have to trade for things we really need for the rest of our journey and I must say it is a very expensive way of buying things!'

Grandfather agreed when he heard the price of a piston.

'One *tael* of gold for a piston!' he looked amazed. 'It's even dearer than the ducks we bought.'

'It's a question of how much we need the piston really,' father replied.

'Well,' grandfather said rubbing his chin, 'although we'll be able to hug the coast now for the rest of the way, even with favourable winds we'd never be properly safe without the engine. You need to get into shelter quickly if bad weather blows up. Let's see what the others have to say.'

In the end it was agreed that the piston should be bought with gold provided by Hung, which the others would repay when they reached Hong Kong.

Father set off alone at half-past seven to collect the piston. The soldier did stop and question him about where he was going but in the end let him go. An hour later he returned.

'I must say he was such an odd man I was surprised to even find him waiting for me,' father said as he handed Lee the piston which was tied up in an old piece of cloth. 'Black market of course,' he added with distaste for anything vaguely illegal.

'It doesn't matter how we got it,' grandfather said soothingly, 'at least we have it now.'

'This is our old one!' Lee held the cracked piston in his palm. 'He's sold us our own piston, it's useless.'

'The robber!' father said under his breath.

'We should complain to the authorities,' Hung said, fretting about his lost gold.

'It was one of them who sent us to that crook in the first place,' father pointed out. 'No doubt he'll get his share of the money from his uncle, and don't forget we have no real right to be here and the nephew, the immigration official, could make things very difficult for us, not only here but right along the coast. For a start dealing in gold is probably illegal anyway and they might want to know how much more we have hidden away. Anyway, they said we have to leave at dawn.'

'I think you are right,' grandfather agreed, 'we'll just have to learn by our mistakes, won't we my son?' There was a slight gleam in the old fisherman's eyes as he looked at his smart city-wise son. Lee thought his father looked like a little boy as he nodded.

'I'll personally repay the gold, Hung, as soon as I can after I reach Hong Kong,' father said humbly.

'There really is no need,' Hung protested rather half-heartedly.

'I must insist,' father said firmly and Hung looked very relieved.

FIFTEEN

At the next port of call they managed to buy a new piston and Lee was very happy to fit it into the engine because the voyage had suddenly become very easy and monotonous.

'There,' Lee said as he set down his spanner and wiped an oily hand across his forehead, almost sad that the piston was fitted and the diversion it had offered was over. 'Would you like to try it grandfather?'

The old man took hold of the handle and swung it. He managed a weak half-swing before he fell back against the cabin-wall, breathing hard, clutching his thin chest and looking very pale and drawn.

Lee was shocked. Grandfather had always seemed the strongest and fittest man on the boat despite his age. 'What is it?'

'Nothing,' the old man gasped, 'just the heat in here. I'll be all right in a moment if I just sit down.' He more or less slid down the wall, using it as a support, and ended up sitting in an untidy heap still gasping for breath.

'Shall I get father?'

'No. You start the engine, make sure it works.'

Lee swung the handle and the engine burst into life.

'Good boy.'

'Is there anything I can do for you?'

'Get me some water, Lee.'

Water was no longer rationed and Lee returned with a full rice-bowl to find that grandfather had heaved himself out into the fresh air on the deck. The old man sipped it.

'I think it is just the heat, nothing more. This has been a long voyage for a man of my age and it has taken a great deal out of me. Don't mention this to anyone, your parents would only worry and there is no need. You can leave me now, I'll be all right.'

Lee did as he was told, although he really felt he should have told somebody about his grandfather's illness. When they put into port in the evening Lee overheard the old man asking one of the local fishermen if there was a *feng-shui* man in the village.

The only reason Lee could think why grandfather would want to see a fortune-teller was the illness. So it was obvious that grandfather hadn't stopped worrying.

The fisherman looked around anxiously. 'The authorities don't approve of such superstitious nonsense,' the man said.

'I do understand,' grandfather nodded.

'But I do know of someone who might help. . . .'

At that point they drifted out of Lee's hearing but next morning when grandfather quietly left the boat Lee decided to follow him.

At last he saw the old man turn in under a square gateway set in a crumbling stone wall. Lee heard the old man knock on the door and the door open and close before he himself peeped into the dusty, paved courtyard set in front of a prosperous-looking house which had a little balcony on the upper floor. There was a huge magnolia tree outside and Lee decided to conceal himself beneath it.

As he sat there waiting Lee couldn't help thinking how odd it would be to start living a perfectly normal life again. This thought was encouraged not only by the men and women who went about their business but by a boy of about his own age who passed by the open gate, obviously on his way to school.

Although it was only about two weeks, to Lee it seemed years since he last went to school. He thought about his old friends and began to get very homesick, then he wondered if they had schools in refugee camps. If they were going to America, as father said they were, he would have to learn to speak the language. Perhaps his father and mother would have to go to school to learn it too, Lee giggled at the thought. But then what would happen to his grandparents? Surely they were too old to learn a new language, but if they didn't what would happen to them?

At that moment the door opened and grandfather stepped out into the sunny courtyard. Lee scrambled out from under the low candelabra branches of the tree and ran towards him. 'What did he tell you?'

Grandfather looked a little annoyed when he realised that Lee had followed him but he was touched by the boy's concern. 'It is good news. Like I told you, there is nothing to worry about. He suggested that I should get something made up at the herbalist but he said that I will see Hong Kong in spite of my little illness yesterday.'

Relieved by the good news Lee enjoyed the visit to the herbalist down near the quay. He was always fascinated by the hundreds of wooden drawers behind the counter which bore labels that included leopard's bone and weasel's liver. He watched with great interest as the herbalist took evil-looking ingredients from several of the drawers. He first weighed them on a little brass hand-held balance before grinding them up with a pestle and mortar. An exotic aroma leeched into the air, which was already heady with musk, liquorice and dried sea-weed.

He put the powder into a twist of paper and handed it to grandfather. 'Just a pinch on your food each day,' he instructed.

As they stepped back into the bright light of the street, Lee couldn't help wondering what his father would think about grandfather visiting a *feng-shui* man or even a herbalist. Yet Lee knew that grandfather wouldn't have set out on the voyage at all in the first place without consulting a *feng-shui* man, just as he had all his life about all important decisions.

They bought a hank of sausages on their way back to

wave about as an explanation for their long absence but nobody seemed to have missed them or even noticed grandfather slip away while they were eating to add some of the mystical powder to his food.

After the meal mother produced a present for Lee.

'What is it? he asked eagerly and was disappointed to discover it was only two shirts.

'The way you've been getting rid of shirts lately, you'd be arriving in Hong Kong without one if I hadn't bought these,' mother said with a smile, remembering the one he'd used to stuff up the leak and the one he'd burnt on the beach which had led to their eventual rescue.

Lee thanked her and although he would have been glad of something more interesting, like a radio, he decided he would wear one of the new shirts straight away just to please her.

He was still wearing it that afternoon when they set sail and he was on watch on the cabin-top. There was much more to see as they travelled along the coast. People on passing ships waved to them now instead of ignoring them.

'I like your new shirt,' Chi said as she scrambled up beside him.

'Thanks,' Lee mumbled. They hadn't seen so much of each other since they'd reached the coast.

'We're nearly there now.'

'Grandfather says another two days and we will be.'

'I wonder what it will be like? I mean we've all been wanting to get there for so long it's become a bit like Tam's dragons, real because we believe in it. What if we don't like it when we get there?'

'We don't have any choice now do we?' Lee said. 'It's not as if we could go back again even if we wanted to. Anyway we won't be there long. My father says they are only transit camps and all the refugees end up some-where else, in another country.'

'Where are you going?'

'My father says America, what about yours?'

A cloud passed over Chi's face. 'I don't think they mind where they go. I hope we go to America too and that we stay in the same camp as your family.'

Lee couldn't help blushing at what amounted to a confession of affection.

'Chi,' he said slowly, 'there's something I've wanted to tell you for some time.'

'Yes?'

'It's about Quan.'

Chi, who had been expecting a different kind of confession looked downcast. 'What is it?'

'Do you remember how ashamed he was of falling asleep on watch that night the cargo vessel almost collided with us?'

Chi nodded. 'He never said anything but I know he was very upset about it because he thought he'd let everybody down.'

'Well,' Lee continued uncomfortably, 'what I never told him, or anybody else, was that I fell asleep too and it was only an accident that I woke up first. When everybody started to treat me like a hero, saying I'd saved the boat, I didn't have the courage to tell them. But when your brother was drowned I was very sorry that he'd died without knowing the truth.'

'Thank you for telling me that,' Chi said. For an instant she rested her cool, long fingers on Lee's hand and he almost wished he hadn't told her after all. Then he looked up and was astonished at what he saw ahead. From the mainland a thin, long, narrow bridge reached out towards a tiny island.

'Trinh!' he shouted, 'Look ahead.'

'That's the Taipa Bridge, we've reached Macao!' Trinh shouted back and everyone stood up to get their first glimpse of the graceful, latticed arch as it appeared through the heat haze.

Everyone except grandfather. He was busy reading a two-day-old newspaper they'd picked up at their last port of call.

'Don't you want to see, grandfather?'

'I'll see it when we go under it, Lee.'

Noisy celebrations went on until a Marine Police patrol vessel met them with immigration officials on board it.

'Are you bound for Hong Kong?'

'We are,' Trinh, their spokesman on all such occasions, replied.

'Good. It isn't that the Portuguese Government doesn't welcome you to Macao but we believe it would be in your own best interests to proceed to Hong Kong if your boat is still seaworthy. Do you have any sickness on board?'

'None,' Trinh answered.

'What about supplies?'

'We want food and water. We also need fuel for the engine. We have money, we can pay.'

'Everything you need will be brought to the boat. Everybody must stay on board and you depart for Hong Kong at first light. Follow us in and we'll show you where to tie up.'

The patrol boat performed a graceful arc in the blue water and the fishing-boat followed in its wake through the maze of sampans and junks that filled the bay. It led them to the Marine Police H.Q. quay which was surrounded by a high wire fence at the gate of which guards were posted.

Adequate supplies of everything they needed were soon brought to the boat although no choice of food was offered. The water bottles were topped up for them and fuel, they were promised, would be delivered in the morning. When they offered to pay for the things they received it was waved away.

'You pay tomorrow,' the men said.

'It seems,' said grandfather, 'we are as welcome in Macao as we were in China. They are willing to help us leave as soon as possible.'

137

'It might be the same in Hong Kong too,' Lee frowned at the awful possibility.

'I've heard it said that the Hong Kong Government has never turned away a Vietnamese refugee boat,' grandfather said confidently.

'Just think,' mother said, as she handed them their rice-bowls, 'the next evening meal we shall eat will be in Hong Kong.'

'It doesn't seem possible we've only been at sea for two weeks,' father added.

'It feels more like two years,' Tam said and everybody laughed.

'I can't wait to get ashore and stay there this time,' Kim said firmly.

'What's the first thing you want to do when you get there?' father asked.

'Write to Dong,' Kim replied without hesitation.

'I thought you'd forgotten all about him,' mother said with surprise, 'you've only mentioned him once during the voyage.'

'No, but I've thought about him. During some of the worst times like during the typhoon and when we were shut in under the deck I thought about Dong. I think that if I hadn't it would all have been unbearable.'

They fell silent for a moment as they all remembered those dreadful times. Then mother, seeing the disapproval on grandmother's face at the mention of Dong, asked her what she most wanted to do when they reached Hong Kong.

'Sleep in a proper bed,' she said without the trace of a smile. They all marvelled that this old woman treated the whole terrible voyage merely as a source of discomfort.

Long after the noises of Macao had died away that night, even the multi-coloured lights of the gambling casinos had been extinguished, Lee was still lying awake thinking back over everything that had happened to them since they left Vietnam.

Thirty-five had set out on the five-hundred-mile journey. Of those only thirty-one would arrive in Hong Kong plus the North Vietnamese they'd picked up during the typhoon. Quan and Khai had certainly been drowned, Khai murdered by the pirates really. Phan hadn't been able to endure the journey. Lan would almost certainly never be seen alive again.

Apart from Khai, who had in a sense brought his misfortune on himself by trying to conceal the gold, all the people who had died were such innocent people. A nurse, a twelve-year-old boy and a baby. Lee's mind dwelt on them and on the thousands of others who must have lost their lives in the same way. Trying to find a new life in a new country they had died.

Lee also remembered what Chi had said about bravery being doing the best you can in the circumstances and he couldn't help thinking that for her, and indeed for most of them, the bravest thing they had done was to take the shortest step, which had been to get on the boat at all.

SIXTEEN

The next day was bright and clear. Everybody woke early, anxious to be off. Tam and the other little ones raced up and down the boat in sheer excitement, getting in everybody's way.

As soon as the fuel was delivered Trinh wanted to know what they had to pay for everything that they had had.

The man looked puzzled. 'But you paid last night.'

'No,' said Trinh,' he said we should pay today.'

'He told me you'd paid, I can't take any more money.'

Trinh shrugged politely. It was clear they were being given everything free to make sure they didn't stay.

'Have you got everything you need?'

'Food and water for one day, it seems very odd that we need so little and yet only a few days ago we had the same quantity on board with no prospect of getting more.'

'You'll get everything you need tonight in Hong Kong. Good sailing!'

As they cast off the ropes from the quay the man waved to them and they all waved back. Although it was early the harbour was full of sampans, junks and larger cargo boats all anxious to be about their business and Trinh had to keep his wits about him to avoid colliding with them. But at last they cleared the harbour and began making their way alongside the long stone causeway that ran out to sea for several kilometres.

'Look!' shouted Tam pointing back towards Macao, 'what's that?'

She was pointing at a huge object on the other side of the causeway which was about to overtake them.

'Is it a flying-boat?' Lee asked.

'No,' father shook his head, 'it's a hydrofoil. Like us

it's bound for Hong Kong.'

It whooshed past sending up sheets of fine spray as it skimmed along the surface of the sea. Lee felt the spray drift across his face as he looked longingly at the fast-disappearing craft. 'I wish I was on that, I bet it'll be in Hong Kong in a couple of hours and we've got to wait all day to get there!'

Even as he spoke their engine coughed and died. There was no breeze at all so they quickly came to a halt, bobbing about freely in the water.

'Get that thing going, Lee!' Trinh shouted. 'Without it we'll never get to Hong Kong at all. And we're sitting helpless in the middle of a shipping lane!'

Lee clambered down below, cleaned out the carburettor and swung the handle. The engine started but during the day broke down three more times.

The hydrofoils plied back and forth as the little boat chugged along a few kilometres at a time. A huge ferry boat overtook them, also bound for Hong Kong, but its passengers gave them no more than a casual wave. Vietnamese refugee boats were a common sight to them.

Their midday meal passed almost unnoticed. Nobody was much interested in eating. Excitement was being tinged with apprehension.

'That engine's brought us all this way, surely it isn't going to fail us now,' father muttered as it coughed and died yet again.

Lee got it going again but hopes of reaching Hong Kong before nightfall were beginning to fade. When they passed a large island Trinh suggested they should tie up there for the night and go on the following day but everybody pleaded with him to go on.

As clouds gathered overhead, they began to think they had made the wrong decision until Hung shouted out that he could see land ahead with tall buildings on it.

'It's Hong Kong,' shouted Trinh, his face streaked with tears. 'It really is Hong Kong.'

It lay under a leaden sky. Victoria Peak was shrouded

in mist. A wreath of drizzle dampened their smiling faces but to them it looked like the promised land.

'I never really thought we'd make it,' father said very quietly. 'I thought it was just a dream.'

A Marine Patrol vessel, tipped off by the captains of the ferry boat and the hydrofoils, was coming out to meet them as it had met hundreds of other similar boats. The procedure was all laid down. Escort the boat to the Western Quarantine anchorage where they would stay for a fortnight before being processed through immigration and sent to one of the transit camps. In six months or maybe a year these refugees, like the thousands before them, would have passed on to America, Canada, Australia or perhaps Europe. Just a matter of routine.

Lee felt there should be fanfares of trumpets or something to herald their arrival.

Tam was leaping up and down. 'Don't forget, Lee, you promised to buy me a doll.'

'I haven't forgotten,' Lee said with a smile. In the distance he could see the skyscrapers on Hong Kong island.

'Grandfather, come and look,' Lee said. He turned to the old man who throughout the celebrations had remained squatting on the deck obstinately whipping the end of a rope they would no longer need.

'Help me up,' grandfather said, laying the rope aside, 'my legs are cramped from sitting too long.'

Lee put his arm under the thin shoulders. 'Look, you can see the skyscrapers and everything!'

'Yes,' the old man said nodding slowly. 'It looks very big. I'm not sure what an old fisherman like me will feel like in a place like that. It isn't like my old village is it?'

'I don't suppose we'll be there long,' Lee said, 'before we go to America like Dad said.'

'That would be good. I expect they have fishermen in America too.'

'Of course they do,' Lee said perplexed by this sudden pessimism from grandfather, then he felt the old man slump in his arms.

He didn't have to look, he knew the old man was dead. Lee laid him gently down on the deck of the boat the old man had brought them in safely to Hong Kong. The *feng-shui* man had been right, grandfather had seen Hong Kong and now his eyes were closed for ever.

Later that night as they bobbed about at anchor, not on solid ground as they had hoped, Lee looked at the glittering lights of Hong Kong. The officials had left them food and water and taken grandfather's body away. They had completed the first stage of their journey which in the end would take them to the other side of the world.

Dampened by drizzle Lee plunged his hand into the pocket of his jeans and found the stump of chewing gum he'd been saving for this moment. Slowly he unwrapped it and put it in his mouth. He chewed it only to discover he'd kept it too long, it had lost its flavour.

A Selected List of Fiction from Mammoth

While every effort is made to keep prices low, it is sometimes necessary to increase prices at short notice. Mandarin Paperbacks reserves the right to show new retail prices on covers which may differ from those previously advertised in the text or elsewhere.

The prices shown below were correct at the time of going to press.

☐ 7497 0978 2	**Trial of Anna Cotman**	Vivien Alcock	£2.50
☐ 7497 0712 7	**Under the Enchanter**	Nina Beachcroft	£2.50
☐ 7497 0106 4	**Rescuing Gloria**	Gillian Cross	£2.50
☐ 7497 0035 1	**The Animals of Farthing Wood**	Colin Dann	£3.50
☐ 7497 0613 9	**The Cuckoo Plant**	Adam Ford	£3.50
☐ 7497 0443 8	**Fast From the Gate**	Michael Hardcastle	£1.99
☐ 7497 0136 6	**I Am David**	Anne Holm	£2.99
☐ 7497 0295 8	**First Term**	Mary Hooper	£2.99
☐ 7497 0033 5	**Lives of Christopher Chant**	Diana Wynne Jones	£2.99
☐ 7497 0601 5	**The Revenge of Samuel Stokes**	Penelope Lively	£2.99
☐ 7497 0344 X	**The Haunting**	Margaret Mahy	£2.99
☐ 7497 0537 X	**Why The Whales Came**	Michael Morpurgo	£2.99
☐ 7497 0831 X	**The Snow Spider**	Jenny Nimmo	£2.99
☐ 7497 0992 8	**My Friend Flicka**	Mary O'Hara	£2.99
☐ 7497 0525 6	**The Message**	Judith O'Neill	£2.99
☐ 7497 0410 1	**Space Demons**	Gillian Rubinstein	£2.50
☐ 7497 0151 X	**The Flawed Glass**	Ian Strachan	£2.99

All these books are available at your bookshop or newsagent, or can be ordered direct from the publisher. Just tick the titles you want and fill in the form below.

Mandarin Paperbacks, Cash Sales Department, PO Box 11, Falmouth, Cornwall TR10 9EN.

Please send cheque or postal order, no currency, for purchase price quoted and allow the following for postage and packing:

UK including BFPO £1.00 for the first book, 50p for the second and 30p for each additional book ordered to a maximum charge of £3.00.

Overseas including Eire £2 for the first book, £1.00 for the second and 50p for each additional book thereafter.

NAME (Block letters) ....

ADDRESS ....

....

☐ I enclose my remittance for ....

☐ I wish to pay by Access/Visa Card Number ☐☐☐☐☐☐☐☐☐☐☐☐☐☐☐☐

Expiry Date ☐☐☐☐